BROTHERS DIVIDED

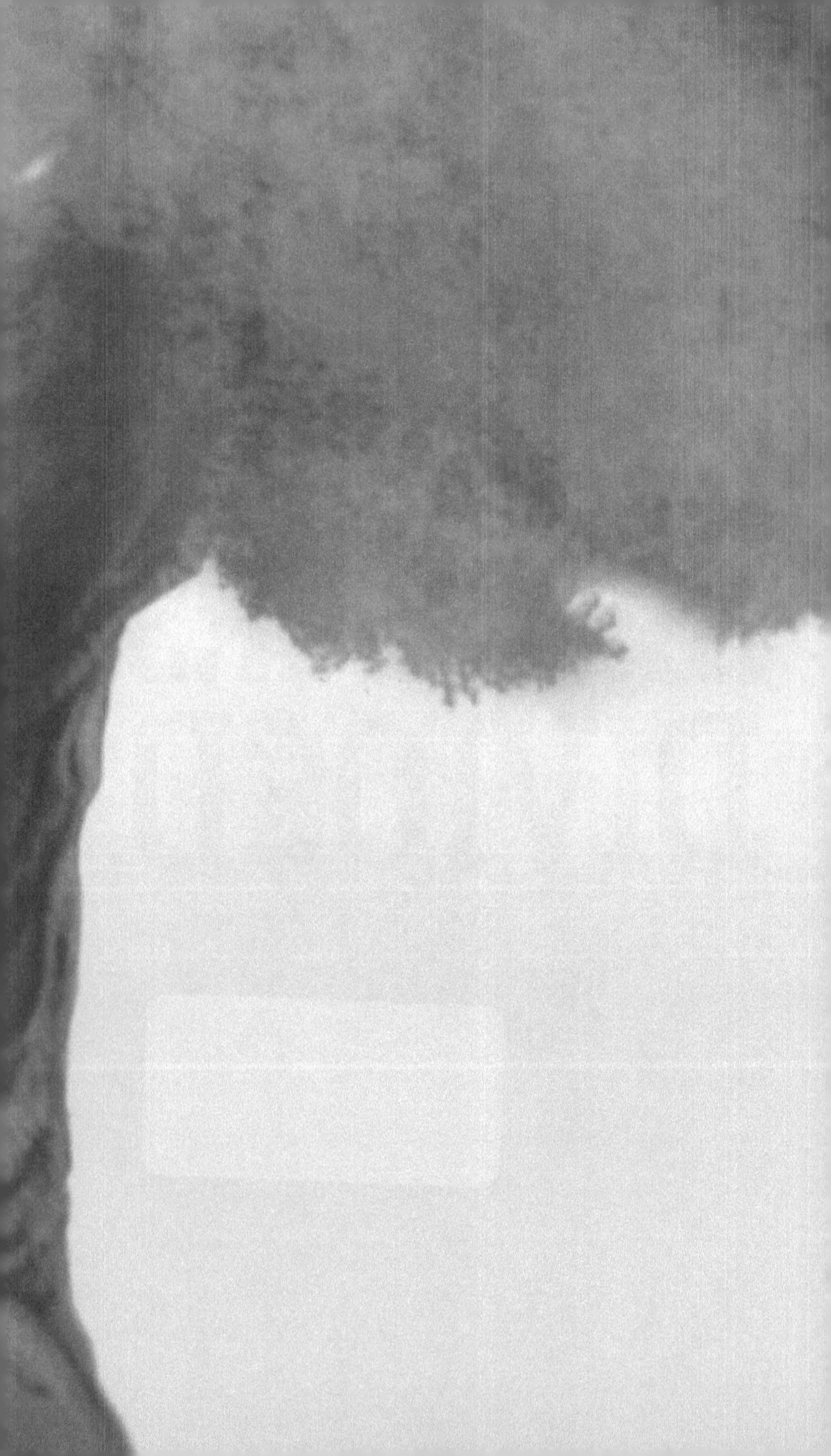

BROTHERS DIVIDED

PC NOTTINGHAM

Published By: The Little Horsemen an imprint of 4 Horsemen Publications, Inc.

The Little Horsemen Publications
℅ 4 Horsemen Publications, Inc.
PO Box 419
Sylva, NC 28779
4horsemenpublications.com
info@4horsemenpublications.com

Cover Illustration by Oxford
Cover Typography and Typesetting by Autumn Skye
Edited by Tabitha Saletri

Library of Congress Control Number: 2025941739

Paperback ISBN-13: 979-8-8232-0941-0
Hardcover ISBN-13: 979-8-8232-0942-7
Audiobook ISBN-13: 979-8-8232-0943-4
Ebook ISBN-13: 979-8-8232-0940-3

DEDICATION

This series is dedicated to all of the children caught in the crossfire of adults who can't put aside their differences, especially the siblings divided by war.

CONTENTS

ACKNOWLEDGMENTS

There are so many amazing people to thank for their support in bringing this series from a crazy idea into your hands: all of the wonderful people at 4HP who took a chance on me, Monique Bucheger, N.C. Scrimgeour, D. Everett Thomas, KC Woodruff, Kathrin Spinnler, Jaci Lunera, Martha Flick, Alex Bree, Elise Edmonds, Nico Vincenty, Hanna Day, Loren Huxley, Mick Vernant, Karim Ragab, N.E. White, AJ Braun, Tiffany O'Haro, and the whole Cru at the Radio Freewrite podcast (WebEater, Krispy, Murph, The Lotus, and Spud). They're all amazing creators and worth checking out!

MAIMON'S NOTES ON THE REGION OF QAWAR FOR THE USE OF NASALID THE LIBERATOR

My dear Nasalid, at your request I have augmented your scouts' reports on this region. Some of this may be known to you, but you demanded thoroughness, and my wife demands I stay on your good side.

PLACES OF NOTE:

- ZelZaytun, renamed Olihort by the Frenglese invaders: the holy city, where all the great founders and heroes of the three faiths have trod. It is home to the holy Gnaverwood tree. It seems that our faiths can agree on only a few things, but two remain constant: there is one All-Planter, and ZelZaytun is the holiest city in the world. (And for the sake of thoroughness, my people once styled the city Ilha Melek back in the Kings Age. Rumor has it my own ancestors conquered it from another tribe, but that, I am afraid, is where history and myth become indistinguishable.)

- The Olive Gnaverwood, ah yes, the sky-piercing goliath, a tree planted by the All-Planter Himself at the beginning of the world. While no rodent could possibly measure it, it is tall enough to act as a sundial for the whole island. Other Gnaverwoods exist on most other big islands I know of, yet this ranks among the largest according to anyone who has taken the time to measure the shadows. Thank the All-Planter only the lowest branches produce olives, otherwise they would be fragrant meteorites when they fall.

- Castle Kraksnout. Both Sprouters and Grovekeepers warn of the wicked going to the Droughtlands after they die. If you permit me, I find it ridiculous that the All-Planter would do such a thing. But if I did believe in such a place, I would believe Castle Kraksnout to belong to it. That grim fortress is built into a hillside, and it is the most impressive fortification I have ever read about. A stocked garrison there could withstand and repel a siege from an army one hundred times as massive.

- Rattin, a crossroads town. Your scout, Kashdood, heard there's a scholarly prayer warden here, so I suppose you'll find it interesting for that. There is also a sheltercake bakery there, but I won't try it. If it's not my grandmother's, it can't be up to snuff. Anyway, what is notable here is that it has two rocky outcroppings near the town. They're known as the 'horns of Rattin.' If you can lure Lady Marjitay's forces here, I suggest a pincer maneuver, but you are more versed than me in such matters.

- There are other villages and towns, of course, but they have come under your influence already, sire. All we had to do was announce that you were an enemy to the Freng and they joined. Or perhaps it was that nasty little rumor about you butchering the nobles who resisted you.

THE RELIGIONS ON QAWAR:

- Mulchers: I list my own faith first, not from some pompous preference, but because we came first in history. We are born into the faith. I'd dare say Mulcherism is not a religion, but a family. But as history has trudged forward, our numbers have dwindled. So few of us twirl the twigs into our beards now, and the upright hairs upon our ears make red squirrels stand out; maybe that is why we are pushed to the side, because we're different. That aside, we believe in the All-Planter, in his divine guidance to King Suleimouse, and we see the great Gnaverwood of Qawar as our sign to plant roots. Ironic how we were pushed out by Sprouters.

- Sprouters: I know you say not to call them the enemy, and the logical part of me agrees with you, Nasalid, but it is hard for me to think of them without remembering my parents, dead at their paws. But that aside, they believe Ganan was the All-Planter's greatest and final Gardener, and he instructed his followers to plant the holy tree's olives throughout the lands of the Great Sea, and to eat olives. Unlike Mulchers, their faith is not bound to one species or culture. Sprouters in Qawar speak Qawari and dress like their neighbors, as the Sprouters in Freng do with theirs. They have a strict hierarchy, with seedlings leading local communities in their "Ganansheds," and saplings managing several seedlings in one area, taking their office in the larger "Gananhalls." They have a single arborist in Gananshire off in Freng. Why the seat of their religious authority is so far from the holy island is a matter I've never understood.

- Grovekeepers: Odd for me to make a description for you since you are one yourself, Nasalid, but you did insist on a thorough report. Well, a group of Sprouters and Mulchers, both dissatisfied with their faiths, convened together and believed that they had discovered the hidden truths which were lacking in the older faiths. They accepted Ganan as a good rodent, but denied the use of his holy rake. They kept the Mulchers' diet but shunned the practice of keeping it to one species. They observe prayers based on the time of day like Mulchers and will periodically fast like the Sprouters. Unlike the Sprouters, with their hierarchy, the Grovekeepers' local prayer wardens do not have an overarching spiritual leader beyond the Divine Poetics. One would think with so much in common with each other we'd have fewer problems, but I suspect that is a problem with rodents and not the All-Planter. Perhaps if we were more different, we'd be more tolerant, but what does an old squirrel like me know?

LANGUAGES SPOKEN ON QAWAR:

- Qawari: a tongue shared by Mulcher, Sprouter, and Grovekeeper across the holy island. It is considered a privileged language by Grovekeepers because of your belief that the All-Planter chose this language for what you call the final revelation.

- Frenglese: a language spoken throughout the Freng archipelago. That and Sprouterism are what unites the rodents of those islands, since they have more kings than they know what to do with.

1

SANU

Under a Gnaverwood's canopy, everyone has the chance for greatness. Only the bold take it.

*- General Ironseed's speech
before the Battle of Batina*

Wispy clouds stretched thin across the sky, fluttering the foreign flag that flew over the holy city of ZelZaytun. Long banners ran down the city walls, displaying the Sprouters' presence. The invaders.

Two squirrel brothers laid down their shovels beside the freshly dug graves, dealing with the reality that their parents were truly gone. Desperate to hide the tears trickling down his muzzle, Sanu turned away from the cityscape and gripped his father's scimitar in both paws.

It was too heavy for him to swing like a proper swordsrodent, but one day it wouldn't be. He'd slice it across the battlefield, helping a great conqueror retake the sacred grove in ZelZaytun. He pulled Jab, his twin, to stand beside him atop the hill, overlooking the thin cedar forest near their hometown.

With a practice swing, Sanu almost knocked himself off-balance, almost stumbling onto Mom and Dad's grave.

"Careful!" Jab cried as he jumped away.

Sanu dusted himself off. "It's the Sprouters who should be careful."

Jab tsked, pulling his head coverings over his eyebrows to avoid seeing the olive tree poking over ZelZaytun's walls. "You can't mean that. You wanna be like them? There's a city full of killers in there."

Sanu averted his eyes from the holy tree—the Gnaverwood—more out of respect for his brother than any belief of his own. "You know they shouldn't be there. Ruining the tree with their creepy rituals."

"That doesn't mean I think you should introduce them to Dad's scimitar." Jab's bushy brown tail coiled behind him. He'd been crying too. "Not like you could slice a whisker with that antique."

"Watch it. What good is *wanting* the Sprouters to leave the city without *doing* anything about it?" Sanu leaned closer, feeling his ears twitch.

Jab wrinkled his snout, making his whiskers wiggle. "I'm doing plenty."

Sanu peered around his shoulder; Jab had their mom's prayer rock curled in his bushy tail. "By praying?"

"Prayer has power."

"So do swords." Sanu hitched the scimitar to his back scabbard with a heave. "Sprouters only speak that language."

"Sprouters pray too."

Sanu scowled and brushed past his brother. "Then you'll enjoy living under their hindpaws." Jab had prayed the whole time Mom and Dad were sick, and look where that got them. Sanu kept that comment under his muzzle though.

"Is this how you wanted today to go, Sanu?" Jab's words made Sanu pause. "Arguing again?"

Arid grass shivered under the breeze.

Sanu turned slowly to face Jab. "Just like Mom and Dad did. It's all we know."

"I guess we're both on edge." Jab's whiskers drooped. "I'm sorry. I don't want to be too much like them, do you?"

Their parents' gravestones were a pair of obelisks they didn't have the skill to carve properly. "Only in the good ways." Sanu's eyes stung and he had to look away. An invisible raindrop got in his eye or something.

Jab offered his paw. "Will the future soldier agree to a truce?"

"How about an alliance?"

With shaky voices and watery eyes, they retrieved their shovels, side by side.

A short walk through shorter grass would bring them to Rattin, their hometown. Jab had the idea to bury their parents outside ZelZaytun's walls so their bodies could rest in the great olive tree's shade—broad enough to block the sun at noon, tall enough to encase their town in shadow for hours at a time.

As they passed their boarded-up parents' home, it felt like the shadow might never leave.

A shopkeeper had agreed to board the boys until they came of age, in exchange for their labor polishing and selling his glassware. He'd given them the day off and a cart for their parents' bodies, since the funeral ritual forbade him from joining them.

"Jab," Sanu said, "even though Mom and Dad argued a lot, do you think the All-Planter will let them into the Walled Garden?" He looked at the sky, blinking away a tear at the thought of his parents in the afterlife.

"On Pruning Day," Jab answered, "nobody gets in right away, except for the honored. A bad fever doesn't exactly qualify."

"But on Pruning Day, do you think they'll get in?"

"We can't know what the All-Planter will do. Otherwise—"

Sanu tsked. "What's the point of spending the whole day with your snout in the holy book if you can't answer these questions?"

"Fair enough. The most repeated passage in the book is that All-Planter forgives. I think Mom and Dad were honest rodents who did their best and made mistakes. That's forgivable, right?"

Jab's pace had slowed, so Sanu took shorter steps to let him catch his breath. "I'm sorry I made fun of you praying."

"Thanks. I bet you'll be a great protector one day."

They crested another hill, which revealed Rattin's prayer house. The trade road bisected the town, and the stores and shops huddled around it with the homes behind them.

The businesses crowded tight to the road so caravans and traders would have to slow down. They'd be caught by the scent of amazing sweets and savories if coming from the west and tempted by a warm bed if coming from the east. A nice town to get trinkets, a meal, or essentials, but not the place twin squirrel boys would want to spend their lives. And the town certainly didn't feel as nice now that their parents were dead.

They both had their eyes on ZelZaytun.

Sanu nudged Jab with his free paw. "Do you think next time you pray with the warden you could ask my question about Mom and Dad getting to the Walled Garden?"

Jab smirked. "I already did. I told you what he told me."

A throaty voice called out, "Back already?" Rijat, the grizzled gerbil who'd agreed to take them in, met them at the foot of the hill. "I'll take my cart. My nieces are playing castles in the flat stretch over there between the horns." He jabbed his tail toward the two rocky outcroppings outside town, known as Rattin's "horns." "Go play with them."

Sanu pawed the cart handle to Rijat. "Um, that's kind of a kid's game. The way Qala and Mutarra play it, at least."

Jab's eyes widened. "What he means is we should be praying and fasting all day to mourn our parents. Since you were kind enough to give us the day off."

Rijat pushed wide wrists against wider hips. "You're only twelve." His voice held the soft and confused tone of an adult who never had kids but wanted to be nice. "You just buried your parents. Do something less adult today. Go play. Show them how young warriors play castles. At least give Qala a break. She's keeping Mutarra from climbing a horn and falling off. She is probably running out of patience."

Sanu nodded and jogged ahead. Rattin's two rocky hills overlooked the town. Kids would play in the grassy space between the horns while the adults traded and worked. Sanu and Jab had spent most of their days there, and maybe childhood didn't need to end the same day they'd buried their parents.

Huffing to keep pace, Jab asked, "Think the girls will go for our way to play castles?"

"*You* barely will. And I'm not throwing rocks at them, if that was your next question." The distraction from his sadness was nice.

"What's wrong with rescuing a trapped lady in a castle? Or are you worried you'll get the south horn?"

"Calling the hills 'horns' sounds dumb," Sanu teased. "The north horn is best because it gets the better shadow covering in the afternoon. But the girls won't play siege."

A gerbil girl shouted a warning. "Watch for the arrows!"

"Arrows?" Sanu peered around.

In mock heroism, Jab jumped in front of Sanu and a twig lightly stung his chest.

"We got you!" Mutarra bounded over as fast as her stubby legs would run. "Jab is dead."

Qala—a young teen, a bit older than the boys—smacked her sister with her thin tail. "Don't joke about that with them." She turned to the twins. "Sorry. Uncle Rijat told us what happened this morning. He suggested we should lighten your spirits, and I told Mutarra you'd want to play castles with armies only. No court intrigue."

"That was nice of you." Sanu stepped in front of Jab, who made a show of his fake wound. "So, you're laying siege to the south hill, Mutarra?"

Mutarra collected her twig arrow and winked. "Yes, and you're the evil Sprouters in ZelZaytun. I'm Nasalid." The other hill should've been ZelZaytun, but Sanu didn't need to correct her.

"I thought you were Nasalid's mighty army?" Qala asked.

"I'm both," Mutarra said with kid confidence. "You can be Dad, my most loyal soldier. You have to write a letter after the battle to tell your daughters about it. Their names are Mutarra and Buttbreath."

Jab pantomimed dressing his fake wound. "Sanu will be the one who's really wounded then. He always wants to play Nasalid."

Fighting in Nasalid's army wasn't some stupid childish dream. "Maybe you should pray that Nasalid pays the Sprouters a visit with his armies." Sanu's voice came out icier than he'd intended.

Jab's whiskers stiffened. "I pray he doesn't bring his war here. Innocent rodents will die."

Qala stepped between them. "Nasalid ousted corrupt leaders and warlords. That's what our dad said in his last letter to us from camp. Fighting isn't some glorious thing we should hope happens."

Both brothers backed off. They didn't want a big sister, but having a mediator helped.

Sanu turned to Mutarra. "Mighty Nasalid, I will never surrender."

"Who are you?" Mutarra demanded.

Grinning, Sanu mustered the screechiest voice possible. "I'm the evil Lady Marjitay!" He wanted to add "queen of the island and granddaughter of the conqueror," but he knew Jab would get mad. That was a painful history, and he didn't want to spoil the fun.

Jab jumped beside Mutarra. "Be careful, Nasalid. She's a wily one."

"And I eat children!" Sanu howled.

Mutarra giggled while Jab scoffed. "You'll never beat the mighty Nasalid. Where are your armies?"

Mutarra pointed at each rocky hill. "My doll at the north horn is Lady Marjitay's army and my other doll at the south horn is Nasalid's reformants."

"Reinforcements," Jab corrected. "You're lucky to have two dolls."

"Don't act like we're rich." Qala rolled her eyes. "One used to be mine."

Sanu cast a kind smile at Jab. "Will you join the forces of evil and stop these noble Grovekeepers?"

Whiskers lifting, Jab replied in his donkey voice that Mom hated. "Yes, I am the evil chef who prepares the children for Lady Marjitay!"

Mutarra play-screamed.

While Qala announced her ridiculous role, Sanu noticed a rodent standing atop the south horn, close enough to observe a few details.

Another squirrel. Older than him. Sand and dirt embedded in his fur, like he hadn't bathed in weeks.

Sanu sidestepped from the game and peered up. This rodent, clad in brown leathers, wore the brimmed hat of a military scout, eying ZelZaytun and the sacred Gnaverwood in the distance. Sanu's mouth dried. This scout had a scimitar, not a straight sword like the ones the Sprouter knights used.

Sanu's heart quickened with the wild thought that the All-Planter really did answer prayers: an army of Grovekeepers could be preparing to retake ZelZaytun.

2

JAB

Hear, O rodents! Measure the strength of another's heart before that of their arms. Measure their mind's speed before their legs.

- Divine Poetics

Jab wrinkled his whiskers. He'd finally gotten Sanu out of his arguments and defensiveness, only for him to stare into the sun while they were playing the game Sanu had wanted to play in the first place.

Worse, Sanu made them look bad in front of Qala.

Struggling not to check if Qala watched, Jab tapped Sanu on the shoulder. He even kept up his ridiculous donkey voice. "Um, excuse me,

Lady Marjitay, we have Nasalid at our doorstep. Maybe we should focus on the problem at paw?"

Sanu ran a paw across his scalp, through his messy hair. "Sorry." He pointed up at the southern rocky hill. "Did you see who was up there?"

Jab pushed up his head wrappings, forming them into more of a visor. Rattin lay at the bottom of the hill, a few minutes' run from their spot between the horns.

The gerbil girls peered in the same direction, and Qala shrugged. "I don't know what you squirrels think you see sometimes."

"What was up there?" Mutarra asked.

Sanu huffed when he faced the hill again. "He must've left."

"Who?" Jab asked.

Sanu's nose twitched, like when Mom cooked herb and garlic chicken with yogurt sauce. "A scout. One of Nasalid's soldiers."

"That's ridiculous," Jab said. "He's nowhere near the Sprouters' outposts." Internally, Jab cursed himself. The invaders came from Freng, and they happened to follow the Sprouter religion. Sanu was rubbing off on him and he didn't like it. "He's taking down weaker princes and warlords on the other side of the island. You say so every day."

"Maybe it's them!" Mutarra squealed. "Qala, didn't Dad say in his last letter that he'd see us soon?"

Qala wrapped her thin tail around her sister's shoulders. "He did, but that's the kind of thing people put in letters."

"Soon can mean almost anything. Days or months." Jab intended helpfulness, but a scowl from Qala suggested he'd failed.

"I don't understand you two," Sanu growled. "If your dad said he'd see you soon, and I saw a scout, both of those things together must mean Nasalid is coming. He'll take ZelZaytun back from the Sprouters!"

Jab understood Sanu's frustration. The girls at least still had a dad, but that didn't excuse Sanu's goose-headedness. "The Frenglese who *happen to be* Sprouters," Jab corrected.

Ignoring Jab, Mutarra bobbed her head. "Then we can go see the Gnaverwood up close."

Jab coiled his tail tight. Killing the descendants of invaders wouldn't bring anyone back from the dead. They wouldn't get their parents back, or the grandparents they never met. Mutarra and Qala wouldn't get their mom back. And Nasalid wasn't a man of the All-Planter, just the conqueror of this generation who happened to be a Grovekeeper—he wasn't even from Qawar Island, if the rumors were true. Nasalid wouldn't usher in a new era of peace and faithfulness. Instead, some other conqueror would come in and replace him or his son. Such was the way of things.

But Jab couldn't start another argument with Sanu. Not today. It would displease the All-Planter and disrespect their parents' memory.

Jab sighed. "How about we climb up the north horn and see what's around? Maybe we'll spot an army in the distance. If we think there's something worth checking, we can climb the south horn too. Mutarra, up for a climb?"

"Always," she said.

Jab and Sanu, as squirrels, had an easier go of climbing than the gerbil sisters. This afforded the boys a chance to help the girls climb by offering their tails, but Qala brushed them off.

"I'd race you to the top if I didn't think one of you would be reckless and break a bone in the process. Girls aren't helpless."

Jab fought the urge to tell her it was a squirrel-gerbil issue and not a boy-girl one, but that probably would end worse.

Sanu reached the top first since he wasn't checking his footing before climbing to the next outcropping. Jab focused on leaving his tail as a last-chance rope, just in case Mutarra needed it. She was so small; he regretted this suggestion for all four of them to climb.

Sanu crouched to offer a paw to the others as they summited.

"See anything?" Jab asked.

Qala tutted. "If you saw a scout, he would have come from that way, right? There are no Grovekeeper armies south of ZelZaytun."

Sanu huffed. "Yeah, and if the Sprouters have their way, we'll be saying 'Olihort' instead."

Jab shook his head. The Sprouters' name for the holy city felt disgusting in his ears. He hated hearing it, more because of the implication that ZelZaytun belonged to the invaders than because it was a Frenglese name. "So no army in the distance. I don't think we need to go to the other horn for a better look."

"Unless they're hidden," Mutarra said.

"Don't be silly," Sanu said. "You can't hide an army. The scout must be really far out of the main force."

"Horsey!" Mutarra shouted.

Qala put her paw over her eyebrows and scanned the area. "What are you talking about Mutarra? There's no—"

Clop-clop-clop

Every hair on Jab's body stiffened. He turned around to face the noise.

A Sprouter knight on horseback approached, close enough to tell he was a beaver, clad in armor that reflected the sun like a mirror. His horse wore armor as well, with Lady Marjitay's honking goose-and-crossbow coat of arms painted on the headpiece, matching the knight's chestplate.

The knight looked more like a metal-coated monster than a beaver.

Beside him strutted a squirrel, a teenager a bit older than Qala, sporting foreign Sprouter clothes. The knight spotted them and har-rumphed something in his harsh language, muf-fled further by his helmet. The squirrel glanced up at them.

With a local accent, the tawny squirrel cried out. "Are you safe up there? Do you need help?" The beaver knight said something else, and the squirrel translated. "He can use his lance like a ladder."

Jab blinked hard. A squirrel from Qawar like them, assisting a Sprouter knight who was clad in armor a demon would wear—helping children. Grovekeeper kids, no less.

Sanu stepped forward, and Jab's stomach tightened. He couldn't let his brother say anything stupid to this knight.

Jab edged in front of his brother, a squeeze on the small plateau. "No, thank you. We climbed up and can climb down. We were just playing. Tell your knight we're safe."

The squirrel translated, and a laugh like Rijat's came muffled through the helmet. The translator called back, "He says he's impressed by your athleticism. He hopes you'll play safe. That doesn't look too sturdy." After a glance at the knight, the squirrel added, "I'll tell him that I played castles on the horns like you did when I was a kid—my mom would always get her sheltercake in Rattin. Nobody back home makes them. If you need help, just shout and we'll come back."

The knight and his translator saluted them and continued toward Rattin. Jab wondered if he'd heard him wrong—could a Sprouter really like to eat sheltercake? How could they appreciate the flaky cheesy pastry straight from the Walled Garden?

"What was that about?" Qala asked.

Sanu's eyes widened. "A Grovekeeper scout and a Sprouter knight, so close together? I think I know what that means."

Mutarra gasped. "A battle?"

Jab surveyed the grassy stretch between the rocky hills. "If there's a battle, I'd rather it's here than Rattin." He looked at his brother and Qala. "We need to warn the townsrodents."

Qala folded her arms. "You're all jumping to conclusions. One knight and one scout are not two armies."

Sanu's whiskers stiffened. "I'll follow that knight. See what he knows."

Jab read his brother's desire to go alone, and knew another way to be a supportive brother. "Hide the scimitar and be careful. I'll check out the other horn and the area around it. I'll see if there are any traces of your scout."

Qala pulled Mutarra close. "And we'll tell Uncle Rijat you both went to do something stupid."

Jab smirked. "What if instead you asked him to read your dad's letter again? Maybe there's another clue in there proving Sanu right?"

"Thanks," Sanu said. Maybe he'd grown sick of arguing too. "Can we agree to meet here at sunset?"

"After the sunset prayer, you mean?" Jab asked. "And see if you can get that beaver to renounce Sprouterism and pray with us. He was nice."

Sanu chuckled. "Yes, and maybe if you have a minute, you could see if Lady Marjitay would peacefully withdraw from ZelZaytun."

"Easy enough," Jab replied. "I'll see you tonight."

3

SANU

Like a fired arrow, Sanu descended the hill that everyone stupidly called a horn and some loose rocks joined him. Maybe it wasn't safe after all. He plodded down the grassier part of the hill as the beaver knight and translator squirrel approached Rattin. While Sanu mostly dreamed of being a warrior, he still needed to practice stealth like a scout.

The knight's concern for Sanu and his friends might have been a ruse. Lure the kids down so he could eat them or sell them. Sanu scoffed at the ridiculous thought. Still, with the stories Dad told about Lady Marjitay, cannibalistic warriors didn't sound too crazy. Especially not after the massacre when the Sprouters from Freng conquered ZelZaytun and renamed it Olihort.

More like Oli-fart.

He chuckled and jogged ahead. The beaver knight's pace was a plodding stroll. Sanu wondered how fast a horse could gallop in a full suit of armor.

Sanu's hair stood on end. Maybe this knight was coming to Rattin looking for a fight. Sanu resisted the temptation to grab Dad's scimitar. An old blade wouldn't do much against polished steel.

Sanu neared the pair, not quite caught up. "Hey, wait!" They had to talk now, enough paces away from Rattin so no wandering ears would notice the conversation.

The knight halted his horse, who whinnied and reared.

Cooing, the beaver patted the horse's neck as he got it to turn around.

The tawny squirrel with the knight cocked an eyebrow. "You're one of the kids from the hilltop?"

Muffled by his helmet, the knight asked the squirrel something, voice trembling with concern.

"Were your friends injured?" the translator asked, mirroring the concern.

"N-no, we're fine," Sanu stammered. "I just wanted to know why you're here."

With his free paw, the knight lifted the snout covering on his helmet, and the glint in his eyes matched the tone in his voice. He said something else, and the translator replied back to him, probably in the Frenglese language.

After the question was relayed through the translator, the knight dismounted. He approached Sanu, towering over him. He reached out, paw inching toward Sanu's head, and Sanu recoiled.

The beaver pulled his paw back and smiled. With a heavy accent, he spoke in Sanu's language. "Friend, teach me Qawar words. Your ... blade is good. You ... like swords?"

Sanu scratched his head, more confused than scared.

"Sir Brouglas is a swordsrodent. He's a collector," the translator said. After a shrug, he added, "and he's been desperate to learn to speak Qawari."

The knight showed Sanu the side of his horse, where a large scabbard poked from the saddle. It looked as long as Sanu's body. "I like swords."

Sanu's pulse quickened. If he could get one Sprouter knight to part with his sword, that would be one less weapon in the push to fight against Nasalid. He could steal it or break it.

And yet, he seemed kind.

Sanu blinked hard. "You're here because you collect swords?"

The translator shook his head. "We're under orders to offer the townsrodents refuge." The squirrel, who could've been Sanu's older cousin for all he knew, glanced back at Brouglas before continuing. "This town might not be safe much longer."

Sanu's heart rose into his throat. "Why?"

Brouglas stomped over, armor clanking with each step. He said something, and the translator gulped.

"Sir Brouglas would like some assistance. Perhaps you and your friends could help us?"

Sanu stepped back and clenched his tail in his hindpaws. "What are you talking about?"

The translator and knight had a quick exchange, worried looks passing between them. "We have reason to believe this town will be attacked by raiders tonight. The Sapling of Olihort will open the doors of the Sacred Gananhall to any who need refuge."

Sanu couldn't remember the difference between a seedling and Sapling, but he knew it was something important in their religious hierarchy and the name Gananhall sounded like a prayer building they used. But the idea of being *invited* into the holy city, the same one his grandparents were killed for living in, wormed uncertainty into his gut.

"Not Lady Marjitay?"

The beaver tutted at the mention of her name, then pointed at her crest on his chestplate. He made motions with his paw as if to say "no," or "don't worry about this."

The squirrel nodded. "Lady Marjitay is in charge of Olihort, but the Sapling can make these kinds of offers. We are working under his orders, not hers. As long as she doesn't command Brouglas otherwise, we can continue." He smirked. "And we made sure nobody knew what we're doing."

Sanu resisted smiling. A kind Sprouter who didn't bow to Lady Marjitay's every whim seemed like something out of a joke. "How do you know there will be raiders?"

"Our scouts found enemy scouts," the squirrel said.

Sanu's fur stood on end. "Most of the rodents in this village are Grovekeepers. There's one family of Mulchers. Will your Sapling force everyone to become a Sprouter?"

The translator relayed the question, and Brouglas' whiskers twitched and eyebrows drew together. The squirrel quickly explained his response. "Of course not. He was upset I didn't know the answer straight away. We won't ask any rodent to renounce his faith. The All-Planter wouldn't take kindly to that."

Hearing the name All-Planter on the lips of a Sprouter felt strange, like watching a squirrel pretend to be a gerbil. He wondered what the Sprouters called the All-Planter in their own language.

Sanu's face hardened. "The rodents of Rattin remember what happened when the Sprouters came to *ZelZaytun* in my grandparents' time. The butchery. Slaughter. Desecration. You might forgive us if we don't want to run back into the paws of Sprouters."

The translator's eyes widened. "I can't tell him you said that."

Brouglas huffed. "I ... understood ... enough."

Bile rose at the back of Sanu's throat. His paws shook to grab his scimitar. He'd go down fighting.

Brouglas unlatched his helmet, revealing a thin cloth around his head, not too dissimilar than Jab's headwraps. "I ... sorry for ... event. I want ... a fix. A sorry. Sapling does ... also." The poor rodent must have been sweltering under that metal and cloth in the midday sun.

The translator spread open his palms. "We believe modern Sprouters of Olihort have a duty to repair our relationship with our Grovekeeper neighbors."

"Nice words, but it's hard to trust a Sprouter." Sanu's throat tightened. But Jab would insist on total honesty if he were here. "Especially an armed one. The adults won't believe you. Nobody will go."

The translator nodded. "You're right, but we have to try."

"How to ... make trust?" the beaver knight asked.

Ideas swirled in Sanu's mind. He could get information from this and offer it to Nasalid. Then the Sprouters would be crushed... or at least driven back into the Great Sea. "Can you show me how a knight fights? I've seen you—well, other rodents—spar and train and run drills outside ZelZaytun. Can you teach me?"

After some relaying, the translator raised an eyebrow. "Brouglas said he could use a new squire and translator after I get knighted, but he'd want permission from your parents. Training you would take weeks before you'd be past the point of hurting yourself, and years before you were useful in battle. He's willing to take you in, but we need a solution to this problem of the incoming raiders today."

An idea emerged in Sanu's mind. "Everyone in Rattin might feel safer if they knew how many soldiers Lady Marjitay had in her army. How many used swords or crossbows... How many armored knights like yourself."

Brouglas smiled. "You sound ... like me." He elbowed the squirrel and said something in Frenglese.

"Sir Brouglas says he heard the rodents around here also played double siege. He said hearing you talk like a strategist, you must play."

Sanu couldn't help the smile forming. Playing double siege with Dad was the closest he could get to learning about military strategy from him. And it was the one game he could beat Jab at. Jab always wasted moves protecting the villagers when he should've been going for the siege engines.

He knew he needed to cherish those memories, but realizing they would never set up their board together again threatened to bring another round of tears to the surface.

Remembering playing the game with Dad twisted his heart, but the prospect lightened his spirits. "I love to play double siege." His whiskers drooped. "But I don't know if anyone will listen to me, even if I think you're telling the truth. If you could beat the bandits in battle, you would show the rodents of Rattin that you knights are protectors, not invaders. Have a host ride from ZelZaytun and defeat them. Have the whole force ride out to show how committed you all are."

The translator placed a finger over his lips and narrowed his eyes at Sanu before translating. "Is there anyone who might believe us?" he asked. "You should take us to someone. We can present the Sapling's offer, but we can't command all of Lady Marjitay's forces."

"Sir Brouglas, what if your translator came with me and you delivered my suggestion to other knights like you? He might have a better chance convincing the townsrodents and gaining their trust without the armor or Lady Marjitay's symbol."

After a quick exchange, the elder squirrel turned to the younger. "He likes your idea. Take me to an elder. Maybe your prayer warden?"

Sanu knew exactly where to take him.

4

JAB

Verily, the Mulchers tell of a city turned to stone by the All-Planter—their punishment for refusing hospitality to a stranger.

- Raticenna's Commentaries

Jab watched his brother trip at the bottom of the horn, but he knew Sanu was fine. He also knew Sanu would get his whiskers twisted if Jab asked.

The gerbil sisters began their descent, and Jab waited until they were both down safely. Not that they needed his help—Qala would rip his tail off if he suggested they couldn't climb.

"I'll see you both after the sunset prayer then, yes?" Jab asked.

"Don't get yourself hurt." Perhaps Qala heard his heart quicken, because she added, "I wouldn't want Uncle Rijat down a stock boy. Who else would get his spare wood?"

Something in how she said "boy" twisted a dagger in his heart, but he shook it off. He was *almost* a teenager, after all. "Yeah, I'd hate to leave him short-pawed. I hope you find something useful in your dad's letter."

Mutarra piped up. "Are you both fine to be by yourselves? Shouldn't you be busy being sad somewhere?"

Qala twisted her ear. "Sorry, Jab."

"It's fine," Jab sighed. "Keeping busy is helping me stay positive today. I know you're asking because you care about us."

"See?" Mutarra stuck out her tongue at Qala, which she promptly grabbed and twisted.

As Mutarra flailed at her big sister, Jab waved goodbye and headed toward the other horn. Bounding across the grassy stretch outside town, he pondered how many children over the years had staged fake battles in this green, using the two rock formations as castles, forts, houses, or boundaries. His parents and grandparents might have. The land gave him a potential connection to them, even if he couldn't know for sure, and something in it lightened his hindpaws. Maybe his parents were still with him in this way.

Jab circled the horn and a set of tracks appeared in the grass. A rodent had definitely walked through here. Yet what kind of scout would leave tracks, especially in grass? It seemed deliberate.

As Jab scratched his head, cold steel touched his chin. By the All-Planter, he wasn't ready to die.

"Make no sound, young squirrel." The voice was masculine and quiet, yet firm. He spoke Jab's language, his accent marking him as an outsider.

Jab breathed deep and slowly pulled his neck away from the blade.

"You one of Lady Marjitay's rats?"

Jab shook his head. A rat? Of all the things to call someone.

The cold steel of a scimitar fell, and the interloper stood before him. A brown squirrel, clad in military leathers, not much older than Qala. He could've been a distant cousin or young uncle. "Those tracks weren't for you to find. I suggest you go home."

Jab blinked hard, staring into the rodent's weary eyes. "Who are you?"

He sheathed his blade but didn't lighten his expression. "Someone who doesn't want to hurt a child. Kids play here?"

Jab struggled to place his accent. He'd probably heard it from a pilgrim or trader at some point. "A little bit ago, my friends and I were playing a game. We don't want any trouble."

The fellow squirrel scrutinized Jab. "You're from Rattin? Not ZelZaytun?"

Hearing the holy city's true name on a foreigner's lips lightened his spirits. Maybe Sanu was right about Nasalid's army. "Yes. I've lived outside the holy city but have never entered. I avert my eyes from the sacred tree."

The scout's gaze flicked to Jab's headwraps approvingly. "And the rodents of Rattin... they're Grovekeepers?"

"All of them," Jab replied. "Except one family of Mulchers."

The scout's eyes widened. "Don't lie to me." A light crossbow hung from his hip—Sanu had always wanted one, but the sight of such a deadly weapon made Jab's skin crawl.

Paws raised and palms open, Jab replied, "I promise, that's the truth. All the Sprouters around here live in ZelZaytun or Kraksnout Castle." Saying the name of the dread knight's fortress reminded him of Sanu's nickname for it of "Crag Snot." He'd never admit to Sanu how funny that was.

"And you've lived here your whole life?"

"Yes." Jab's hair stiffened. Somehow his honest answers felt like the wrong ones.

The older squirrel twitched, and Jab tensed. He stared at the afternoon sky and shook his head. "Listen, there's not much time."

Jab gulped. "Not much time before what?"

"Tell your prayer warden to raise a flag over the prayer house tonight. Beg the All-Planter to give me speed."

"I—I will," Jab stammered.

The scout zigzagged his tail in front of his hindpaws to show respect, then bolted away. Jab had never seen anyone move so fast.

He took the urgency as a hint to run back to Rattin. The warden would know what to make of this meeting.

Dirt and bits of dried grass stuck in Jab's hind-paws as he sprinted through the rolling hills toward Rattin. He needed to apologize to Sanu when he had the chance. He regretted doubting him. Maybe he owed Rijat an apology too. The kind gerbil had only wanted Sanu and Jab to try to be happy today, as if playing together and acting like kids would ease the sting of their parents' passing.

A tear threatened, but Jab blinked it away. Whatever was about to happen to or around Rattin took priority over grieving.

It had to.

Not like his parents would get the afterlife they deserved with the Sprouters blocking the way to the Walled Garden. Jab used the anger to increase his speed. He sprinted between the two houses on Rattin's outskirts. He hopped over his neighbors' pots and ducked under their laundry lines. A scent of cinnamon sheltercake tempted him, but he stuck to his course. Rijat's shop was on his left, but he turned right.

Jab banked around a group of kids Mutarra's age playing in the street, and again to avoid somebody's mom carrying a basket of bread out of the bakery.

His mom would never come home with a basket of bread for their family ever again. He winced at the realization, but pressed forward until he came to the prayer house. The sundial's shadow taunted him.

Jab had missed the afternoon prayer.

His throat tightened. He missed a prayer on the day he buried his parents. He'd barely mourned them. Maybe he was afraid to pray for that reason.

This one omission wouldn't send him to the Droughtlands when he died, but it wrenched his gut. He should have been turning to the All-Planter the entire day.

These tears proved too strong for him.

In the middle of the day, when everyone was out in the streets, here he was, wiping his eyes with his forearm like a toddler.

A gentle paw rested on his shoulder. "Come here for prayers or study today, Jab? I wish you'd play with the other kids though."

The voice belonged to Miai, the warden, a kindly jerboa and the unofficial uncle of every kid in town. Even the one Mulcher family's kids liked him. He'd use his whip of a tail and long hindpaws to hop and dance while teaching the youth how to pray. Though he didn't look like a squirrel, Jab sometimes called him "Uncle."

Jab swallowed a whimper, wiped his eyes again, and stared up at him. Miai's wide ears blocked the sun from Jab's face, offering a for-giving reprieve from the heat.

Collecting himself, Jab managed to speak flatly. "I forgot the midday prayers... I had to get a message to you."

"I see," Miai said without judgment. "This was an important message, yes? So important that everything else was blocked from your mind?"

Jab pinched his tail and stared at his hind-paws. "Yes."

"Perhaps this was the will of the All-Planter, who is more forgiving than you. In His wisdom, the All-Planter commands us to pray, not because He needs it, but because we do. Years ago, my daughter cried through the night during her first weeks. I slept through sunrise prayers many times. I felt horrible, but my teacher told me that the All-Planter knew I needed more sleep to be a better father and warden. Give yourself permission to make mistakes, alright?"

As Jab sighed, the tension left his shoulders.

"Now, let's step out of the sun and you can share this message."

Miai and Jab covered their left ears with their tails and crossed the threshold.

Sunlight poured into the atrium and Miai grabbed a stool for Jab on the polished stone floor. "Can I offer you some water?" The architecture allowed for Miai's voice to echo in a way that became musical.

Jab politely refused, then told him about the scout. Miai listened with rapt attention.

When Jab finished, Miai stomped his long foot. "We'll tell everyone to shutter their homes and shelter inside tonight."

As Jab opened his mouth to agree, his breath caught. He needed to warn Sanu and the sisters not to meet back at the horns at sunset. Only the All-Planter knew what terror would befall Rattin tonight. Jab would turn over every basket to find his brother in the town.

5

SANU

Sanu quickly navigated Rattin's houses and shops with the older squirrel trailing him. The sheltercake bakery tempted his stomach as much as the blacksmith's forge turned it.

"Young man," the translator said, "I never got your name."

No reason to lie. "Sanu, sir."

"I'm not a sir, but thank you. Sanu was my grandfather's name, actually."

Sanu hid his face so the other squirrel wouldn't see his shock.

A Sprouter sharing his name?

Maybe this guy's grandfather was a Grovekeeper and someone along the line renounced the true faith, which wasn't a comfort. He could only imagine what Jab's reaction would be when he told him later.

"Oh," was the only response Sanu could summon. "And your name?"

"Yagub." It almost sounded like a Mulcher name.

"Well, Yagub, I'm taking you to the prayer warden. He's a jerboa named Miai."

"Miai of Rattin? I thought that was a pen name."

Sanu wasn't entirely sure what pen names were, but he wasn't about to sound dumb and ask. "How do you know him?"

"The Sapling asked for local writings about the Grovekeeper faith." Yagub waved his tail playfully. "Like Brouglas and I told you, there are many of us in Olihort who wish to live here as good neighbors. That's only possible with understanding."

This was all so confusing. Sprouters were the reason for the strife in this land. They were blocking the way to the Walled Garden. Maybe his parents' passing added to his confusion, but something wasn't sitting right. His scimitar felt even heavier on his back.

The pair finished their journey outside the prayer house, where Miai chatted with the potter.

At their approach, the graying jerboa twitched an ear. He waved off the artisan and faced them.

"Sanu, you just missed your brother." His tone mixed his usual joviality with a note of urgency. "Welcome to Rattin, young man," he said to Yagub. "Serenity to your family."

"Tranquility to your home," Yagub replied.

It was hard enough to believe there were Sprouters who were native to Qawar, but hearing the correct response made Sanu's eyebrows raise.

Miai smiled at Yagub. "Thank you. May the All-Planter's truth guide you. You've chosen a fantastic guide to take you to Rattin. Am I a stop on the tour or do I have the pleasure of welcoming you into our prayer house?"

Sanu wished the knight had accompanied him instead, and maybe Sanu could have used some code to explain everything to Miai without the drawback of a translator eavesdropping. "Miai, this Sprouter and a knight told me that they believe raiders will attack Rattin tonight."

Yagub nodded. "I've come to invite the citizens of Rattin inside Olihort for safety."

Uttering the hated name made a townsrodent walking past turn and scowl, but Miai's expression remained flat. "Why?"

"The Sapling wants to offer refuge as a gesture of goodwill."

Trying to sound honest, Sanu nodded. "He and his knight aren't like the ones we've heard about." He made sure his tone wasn't like when Miai asked him if he'd prayed enough times on any given day.

Miai folded his arms. "These raiders, what do you know about them?"

Yagub held his paws up, palms out. "Only that they are raiders. Our scouts think they'll attack tonight."

Miai's tail slithered across the pavement. "You wish for us to evacuate our homes to avoid people attacking? We have a right to defend ourselves. Your offer is generous, but misguided. Tell your Sapling I respect his kindness, but these rodents will not leave Rattin."

The translator inclined his head. "You're certain?"

"I am," Miai said with firm kindness. "Loan us weapons if you think we need help defending ourselves. While many of us wish to make a pilgrimage to ZelZaytun, the place you call Olihort, fear for our safety prevents us. That same fear will also prevent the rodents of Rattin from following you anywhere. When many of our parents and grandparents left the city for the last time, it was to escape execution."

Staring at his hindpaws, Yagub asked, "Is there anyone else I can talk to?"

"Yes. Pray to the All-Planter until He reveals enough wisdom for you to understand my words. Sanu, please offer our guest some food and a bed in the inn. Whatever expense is due, tell the shopkeepers to collect the money from me." His eyes flitted back to Yagub. "Unless you need to leave sooner."

Yagub ran a paw through his hair. "I thank you for the offers, but I must return to Oli—the city. My knight needs his translator back."

"Return without weapons and the two of you will feast with us." Miai somehow sounded generous and stern at the same time.

Sanu waved to Miai and coaxed Yagub to walk with him. Rattin's townsrodents passed in both directions, casting glances at each squirrel. If all the Sprouters were like Yagub and Brouglas, the massacre wouldn't have happened. But the possibility also remained that Yagub and Brouglas were the exceptions that proved the rule, and Lady Marjitay was the better representative of the Sprouters. He didn't like sending Yagub away empty-pawed, but Miai had good points.

They couldn't leave themselves undefended, and Sanu didn't have a way to tell Miai the so-called raiders might really be Nasalid's army. Perhaps the knight would have some success in convincing the other knights to ride out and protect Rattin.

After leading Yagub out of town and bidding him farewell, Sanu wondered if he'd see this translator again, and if he'd condemned a group of rodents to death in battle.

Odd how he'd seen two older squirrels the same day he buried his parents. Probably a coincidence, and Sanu wasn't the superstitious type. Jab wasn't either, but he'd have something to say about the symmetry. Sanu's eyes widened—he needed to find him.

A quick glance at the sun told him he didn't have much time to find Jab before they were supposed to meet again at the horns. He couldn't let Jab run around without the full information, especially if that meant running into Nasalid's scout.

Sanu took off at a sprint. He'd turn over every rock outside the town to find him. Jab must be somewhere out there in the surrounding fields.

6

JAB

- *Divine Poetics*

Under a blue-orange sky, Jab resisted the urge to smack the side of the sheltercake bakery.

"He wasn't by the glassblower either," Qala called.

"We should meet him at the horns," Mutarra said.

Jab twisted his whiskers and cringed. "No. You both stay inside. Rijat needs to know you're safe whenever this attack happens."

Qala stomped on the pavement and stared scimitars at him. "Hey dummy, same goes for you. Uncle Rijat needs to know you're safe. Sanu isn't an idiot. If he goes to the horn, he'll see we're not there and come back to the store. This isn't a game."

Mutarra tugged on Qala's sleeve. "Can we please go back to the horns?" Her whiskers drooped.

Jab's eyes widened. "By the All-Planter! Your dolls, Mutarra! You left them at the horns."

She stared at her hindpaws. "They were guarding the castles until we got back."

Qala scoffed. "Well, this will be a great exercise in being more responsible."

"I can't sleep without them." Tears welled in Mutarra's eyes.

A rock formed in Jab's stomach which matched the prayer rock he carried with him, the prayer rock from Mom. His mind drifted to Sanu's scimitar, the one heirloom from their dad. At least the scimitar wasn't a horrific crossbow—those things made Jab's skin crawl.

"I'll get the dolls back, Mutarra," Jab said.

"Like Droughtlands you will," Qala called as Jab sprinted away.

As he tore through the street under lengthening shadows, Miai sounded the call to prayer. Everyone in Rattin, along with Grovekeepers all around the world, would begin the prayers to end the workday. That's what these prayers were for, right? Jab blinked hard as he reached the end of the town. Sunset prayers capped the workday and marked the transition to time with family. His work was not done, and he couldn't be with the only family he had left.

An echo rang from Rattin, signifying the end of the prayer. The hills loomed in the distance, beyond a grassy plateau with rocky outcroppings on either side. Kids played at warfare there because it would be a good place for a real military outpost; the stony formations even resembled castles with a squint and dash of imagination. And beyond that, the horns stood tall enough for someone to see a good portion of the area.

As Jab scrambled upward, a heavy rustle rattled the dry grass on the plateau's other side, yet not even a whisper of wind pushed at his clothes. The plateau and hills didn't seem big enough to break wind apart.

Breathing heavy, he reached the top. The north horn was closer, so he sprinted over to it, legs burning.

Mutarra's doll poked out from the shadows.

Perfect. He just had to push himself a little more.

Clop-clop-clop

Jab's brain screamed for him to stop, but he couldn't dare face the sound.

Clop-clop-clop, cloppa-cloppa-clop

His ears stiffened. Lots of horses.

He dove atop Mutarra's doll, then spun around and scooched backward until his back rested against the rocky horn.

A horde of armored knights approached, carrying the dread goose-and-crossbow banner of Lady Marjitay.

As Jab's breathing quickened, another round of thundering hooves reverberated, shaking loose rocks above him. This time, the hooves were behind.

A band of mounted archers, lightly armored, held high the golden banner featuring a double-headed winged wolf, the same seal he saw on Qala and Mutarra's letters from their dad, the symbol of Nasalid's army.

Sanu had been right—things were about to get very unsafe.

He clutched Mutarra's doll tight to his chest. She'd have to deal with only having one for tonight. But he still had to find Sanu. He couldn't run headlong between these two groups, so his one option was to ascend the horn. Pushing himself to do so quietly, he rose as the groups of horses clopped closer together. Not an all-out charge, but they were preparing to fight.

Once he stood atop the horn, he peered toward the other.

A squirrel stood at the foot of the horn, on the same side as the Sprouter knights, clutching Mutarra's other doll.

The scimitar and ruffled hair made it clear: Sanu was here.

They'd kept their promise to each other, but Jab had no way of signaling to Sanu below. He could only barely make out the doll, but the scimitar marked Sanu as the outsider.

A *thwang* reverberated through the air, stealing Jab's attention. One fiery arrow sailed overhead, careening toward the group of Sprouter knights. The arrow landed harmlessly behind them, in the dried grass. Four more *thwangs* followed, with four more arrows.

A spark ignited in the grass, a candle's flame in one second, spreading into a ring around the entire hill, encircling both horns. In the next second, the candle flicker grew to a torch. Somebody must've poured oil into the dry grass.

A searing heat and roaring blaze erupted like something out of mythology, illuminating Sanu enough for Jab to see him realize what was happening.

This whole thing had been a trap for the knights. And Sanu was right there.

Jab helplessly watched his brother, his last family, engulfed in the fire. As he screamed his brother's name, he lost his footing and fell.

His head connected with a rock, and he rolled down the rest of the climb. The blunt pain in his head intensified every sensation, like his whole skeleton needed to react and spasm.

Stars flooded his vision, and the screams of Sprouter knights filled the air. Jab was at least on the other side of the ring of flames, but their blazing intensity pressed on him.

As he struggled to get on all fours, a pair of paws grabbed him by the shoulders.

"You're the boy from this afternoon."

Jab struggled to meet the scout's gaze.

"You're coming with me. I'll take you to the physician—you need some bandages and medicine after that fall."

As the soldier scooped him into his arms, Jab had no reason or ability to protest. He'd lost everything and everyone. Plague stole both parents, and now his brother had burned to death. The All-Planter promised happiness for rodents who followed Him, and this seemed like a cruel joke.

He hadn't even been a good brother, picking arguments all the time. He'd lost his chance to make amends with his last family. And Jab had nothing to return to.

The Sprouters from Freng had taken everything from the Grovekeepers, killing Jab's grandparents before he could ever meet them. Their desecration of the sacred Gnaverwood blocked passage to the afterlife, denying Jab's parents their much-deserved rest. The occupation of ZelZaytun made Jab's desire to make a pilgrimage there impossible.

If the Sprouters had never arrived and done such horrible things, this battle would never have happened and Sanu would still be alive, swinging his scimitar.

Maybe Sanu had the right idea all along. These colonizers only spoke the language of war. Jab would right the wrongs done against the good rodents of Qawar.

For Sanu.

7

SANU

Our faith teaches us to associate fire with evil. On the contrary, it is a tool.

- Warrior Maxims

A cloud retreated from the setting sun, and the call to prayer echoed from Rattin.

Sanu hustled back to the meeting spot. After peering behind every shrub and rock all afternoon, he still saw no sign of Jab—Sanu had been so sure his twin would've been out here somewhere. The only thing he noticed worth mentioning was a jerboa hopping between the horns with a pot of oil. He didn't think much of it.

With the sunset wind speeding him and rustling the dry season's grass, Sanu bolted back to the Horns of Rattin, a name too cool sounding for boring hills outside their boring town. He scrambled up the south horn and grabbed Mutarra's doll. Staring at the little thing in his paw, he decided if Jab arrived before the girls, he'd let Jab give the doll back to her, impressing Qala for sure. Sanu owed him that for their argument this morning. His parents would be proud knowing he helped his brother. Remembering the morning, he turned to the north horn to grab Mutarra's other doll—only a few minutes' walk. As he left the shade, a muffled thundering made him pause.

He faced the noise.

Clop-clop-clop.

Tall flags and banners appeared from behind the hill.

Clop-clop-clop, cloppa-cloppa-clop

Sprouter knights.

Sanu's ears stiffened. Had Brouglas really gotten a band of knights together to fight the raiders? Were these invaders trying to become protectors?

Then, more hooves sounded from the opposite side.

And there it was: the golden wolf banner of Nasalid the Liberator. The hero, the one who Sanu had dreamed and prayed and hoped would come to shake off the Sprouters from ZelZaytun.

Sanu's heart dropped to his stomach. Brouglas and Yagub were probably in this band.

His mouth dried, and his gaze flitted between the two approaching groups of soldiers. Armored Sprouter knights with lances and longswords marched toward mounted archers.

Thwang!

Sanu gasped at a fiery arrow ripping through the sky.

As he watched it plummet, he saw someone atop the north horn.

From the headwraps and bushy tail, there was no mistaking his brother.

Sanu stepped forward, wondering how to signal Jab without alerting the encroaching soldiers.

Thwang-thwang-thwang-thwang

Four more arrows pierced the sky, hitting the grass in front of him. Sanu stared down and noticed the dried grass had been slicked down.

The jerboa with the oil pot.

Flames crackled in the grass, spreading into a circle. The sound crashed like hail smacking metal. The roaring fire erupted into an inferno, dancing around Sanu.

Through the rising blaze, his last sight was Jab falling down the rocky hill and hitting his head before rolling out of sight. If the fall hadn't killed him, the fire would. It was the dry season after all.

"No!" Sanu had just watched his brother die in front of him. There had to be some mistake. This had to be a joke.

The Sprouter knights charged, oblivious to Sanu, rushing headlong into the mounted archers. Sanu needed to find his brother, so he could at least tend to his body. His whole family was dead and he'd failed to save any of them. Surrounded by rodents, Sanu had never felt so alone and abandoned.

The stench of singed fur assaulted Sanu's nostrils, and a burning pain snapped him back to attention. His hair was on fire!

Sanu dropped to the ground and rolled, igniting some of the dry grass around him. He screamed, barely audible against the fire's noise.

"Sanu!" The voice belonged to Brouglas. A pressure folded around Sanu's body, tamping at the flames. It was a cloak, or something like it.

As the burning pain subsided, replaced by a dull ache, Sanu's vision cleared.

Brouglas hunched over him, extinguishing the flames not with a cloak, but a banner.

Screams, shouts, and death raged behind him, yet Sanu was safe, saved by a Sprouter and a banner with Lady Marjitay's coat of arms emblazoned on it.

With an "oof," Brouglas shoved Sanu onto his horse, which whinnied beside the growing flame wall. Brouglas hopped up himself, taking the position behind Sanu in the saddle. He yanked the reins and his horse galloped away from the fire and battle.

More screams followed and the odor of charred fur and flesh wafted around. Sanu was glad they were descending a hill—he couldn't imagine how much worse things smelled and sounded above now.

Brouglas muttered something in his language, then spoke over the sound of clambering hooves. "Safe... safe... healer I take you to. Safe."

Despite his painful burns and the banner blanketing him, Sanu shivered in the chilly night. "Why did you help me?"

"Battle was a ... trap. A trap. Your friend Brouglas, not like traps. See you in fire. Pull you out."

"Thank you," Sanu squeaked. A Sprouter had risked his life for him, one from Freng, no less. If Brouglas had been a little slower, he would've baked alive in his iron armor with all that fire. Being grateful stung, knowing Jab wouldn't get the same rescue he did.

He still had Mutarra's doll. It wasn't supposed to be like this.

Nasalid had prepared a cunning trap for the Sprouter knights. Brouglas' companions might have all died in the flames. It wasn't an honorable way to fight, yet this spared Nasalid's troops' lives and equipment. No casualties, and only four arrows used. Not a bad tradeoff for a general.

But this battle came at the cost of Jab's life.

Sanu couldn't celebrate a victory which felt like a loss. Even though a Grovekeeper general carried the day and Lady Marjitay suffered a loss of troops, Sanu felt the defeat in his bones. First his parents, now his brother.

And a glance down at the honking goose-and-crossbow banner of Lady Marjitay reminded him that he'd been saved by an enemy, to add insult to the grief.

"Are you taking me to ZelZaytun?" Sanu asked.

"Take you to Olihort."

Sanu wondered if Brouglas saying "Olihort" was a rejection of the city's true name or if he didn't even know and was stating directions. The holy city peeked over the next hill, and its colossal olive Gnaverwood tree defied the clouds. He knew he wasn't supposed to look directly at it out of respect, yet this tree was too awesome not to stare. Sanu wondered if that rule not to look at the tree was because people would stare at it all day.

Jab would know the reason. Or at least, he would have.

Guilt twisted in Sanu's heart again. His pious brother didn't want to die on a battlefield. He didn't want to be involved in any fighting. His brother was a peacemaker, and Sanu's obsession killed him. Jab would've wanted the Sprouters to leave ZelZaytun, but not through violence and death. Maybe Sanu could show the Sprouters another way. One that involved healing of past mistakes and misdeeds. One where the holy city was shared between Sprouters, Grovekeepers, and even the few remaining Mulchers. That's what Jab would've wanted: not allowing Nasalid to conquer the city, but instead creating an environment where nobody felt that he had to. Real dialogue and real peace between the faiths. That would've made Jab happy, and that's what Sanu was prepared to do.

For his brother.

Dad's scimitar pressed into his back. Sanu didn't have to forfeit his dream of being a great swordsrodent. There'd be plenty of bandits and raiders who'd threaten towns once the conflict was over.

And this conflict would end.

It had taken enough innocent rodents from Sanu and countless other kids.

No more.

He had allies in Brouglas and Yagub. That was a start.

8

JAB

Why do the Widow's Poem and the Orphan's Poem stir so much emotion? The All-Planter wants us to extend the greatest generosity and empathy to these, since life has taken so much from them already.

- Raticenna's commentaries

A wet pressure on Jab's head nudged him awake. This wasn't the Walled Garden, that much was certain. And the wet pressure came from cool water on a cloth, which thankfully ruled out the Droughtlands too.

With a deep inhale, Jab opened his eyes to soft sunlight.

The squirrel scout from the day before hunched over Jab, dabbing his forehead.

"Welcome to the world of the wakeful," he said. "How are you feeling?"

Jab wanted to complain about all the loss he'd experienced over the last few days, but he wasn't about to insult this rodent's generosity. "My head hurts. What happened last night?" What he really wanted to ask was if he had truly died, could he see his family?

The scout offered a paw to help Jab sit upright. They were inside a tent. Other rodents, all adults, slept in cots beside him.

"First, it occurred to me last night that we never exchanged names. I was worried if you passed, I wouldn't know who to inform. My name is Kashdood of Sqirlib, named for my father, but everyone in camp calls me Kash. I serve as a junior scout to Nasalid the Liberator." He cleared his throat. "Um, and I'm sorry. I'm probably not helping."

"I'm Jab of Rattin." Unable to say son of anyone, he'd just outed himself as an orphan.

Kash closed his eyes. "I see. Jab of Rattin, perhaps it's a mercy of the All-Planter that you came to us. You see, we cannot allow you back into Rattin. We have to keep our location a secret. We are a good bit away."

Jab exhaled. Rijat ought to know that at least one of the boys placed in his care still drew breath. Yet he couldn't burden that poor man with any more. Maybe he could send a letter.

Kash must've noticed the droop in Jab's whiskers. "I know that may hurt, Jab, but understand, Nasalid's campaign relies on some level of secrecy. You've seen his ambush tactic with the fire. We can't risk the enemy knowing anything."

Jab's fur stood on end. "So... no survivors last night? From the other side, I mean." Maybe Kash would tell him they found one young Grovekeeper squirrel hidden between the Sprouter knights, and Sanu snoozed in another tent nearby.

Kash's tone was grim. "The only survivors are prisoners. Nasalid accepts all surrenders. Any weapons, armor, provisions, or horses accompanying a surrender are given to the troops to sell and provide for their families or restock themselves."

An ailing soldier in the next cot groaned. "It's a disgrace. They eat as well as us."

A few hoarse guffaws followed while Kash shrugged.

This conqueror actually followed the Divine Poetics' rule. Jab wondered how else Nasalid might uphold the faith. Couldn't be too much if he commanded troops to kill.

Kash stood and let Jab grab onto his tail to do the same. "I will be direct. Nasalid requires your service. Our information about this area seems to be faulty or outdated. If I hadn't run into you earlier, we may have attacked Rattin instead, thinking it to be a town of Sprouters and supporters of Lady Marjitay or colonists from Freng."

An image of Mutarra and Qala's father flashed in Jab's mind. "Aren't there soldiers from this part of Qawar?"

"Of course, but..." Kash led Jab outside and dropped his voice to a whisper. "If too many rodents know the general's plans, we risk discovery."

Jab stepped into a row of tents. In between two, a gerbil blacksmith pounded at a forge and a squirrel carpenter mended a wagon wheel.

Neighs and clucks sounded from between other tents. With the mixing stench of animals, aroma of savory breakfast foods, and the chatter of adults, this cluster of tents appeared like a portable city. Nasalid wasn't merely marching an army; he had an entire support system. No wonder he had been so successful.

Caring for animals is virtuous.

Considering the needs of others enough to have a dedicated physician's tent was too. Jab felt silly for never considering an army having these things before, but he'd only ever thought of soldiers as hired killers. Qala's support for her father had puzzled him.

Not that Jab was interested in her. And beyond whatever else he felt, he was certainly jealous she *had* a father.

"First time in a camp, I reckon," Kash said. "It's quite overwhelming, right?"

"That's one way to put it." And that wasn't even considering his throbbing head or the gaping hole in his heart as the reality of losing his whole family solidified.

"The stench from the animals and fires isn't too much for you, is it? I knocked my head once and every smell made me want to vomit."

"No, I think I'll be fine." Jab followed Kash through the rows of tents. Some rodents sharpened scimitars, others tended to horses, many strung bows, and a few intoned their morning prayers. Jab winced. His injury forced him to sleep through morning prayers. That was three consecutive prayer times he'd missed now. He vowed he'd pray three times over the instant he had a moment to himself. If he dropped down to pray now, it would be an act of procrastination to avoid meeting Nasalid, not piety. Using prayer as an excuse would be worse than not praying at all.

One tent loomed over the others, marked by Nasalid's golden wolf banner. Jab approached it, but Kash shook his head and smirked. "That's the decoy tent for the spies to attack. It's the falconer's tent." Kash directed him to another tent, the same size as all the others and equally as unremarkable. "This one is the Liberator's."

"Do spies attack a lot?" Jab wondered how many enemies Nasalid made on his rise to power, and how many of them still lived.

"Not since I enlisted, but Nasalid is precautious."

As they approached, a burly jerboa cut them off, balancing a spear between his paws. "State the password, Kash."

"I refuse." Kash tapped Jab's shoulder with his tail.

The jerboa lowered his spear and stepped aside. "This the kid?"

"Yes," Kash replied. "The savior of Rattin."

Jab's eyes widened. He never wanted to be called that again.

The jerboa lifted the tent's entry flap, revealing a wooden dinner table with an unfurled map on it. Carved marble figurines dotted the map. Three men huddled over it. In the corner, an older red squirrel sat on a small rug, reading.

Standing above with arms folded was a jird, a species he hadn't seen in the camp. This jird was a tall rodent with a neat beard. His head-wraps had two openings for his ears, which bore enough divots and scars in them to make them appear spiked. His thobe matched the other soldiers', but his right sleeve bore slash marks, and chain mail poked through at his wrists. Two older, shorter rodents stood beside him. One, a gerbil, wore headwraps and the same warden's cloak Miai did, and the other, a jerboa, dressed more like a prince than a soldier.

"Lord Nasalid," Kash bowed and indicated Jab. "I bring you Jab of Rattin, the boy who provided us with the information about his town."

The jird pulled his gaze from the map and moved his arms behind his back. His impeccable posture intensified his piercing gaze. "You have my thanks. We were prepared to attack that town to draw out Lady Marjitay's troops. You saved innocent lives." Nasalid's accent marked him as a foreigner, but it didn't match Kash's. "I cannot tell you what a relief that is. We thought Sprouters used Rattin as a supply depot." He didn't slouch, but his tone relaxed. "I have a gift for you, young Jab."

Nasalid opened a drawer under the map table and pulled out Mutarra's doll. "This was clutched in your paws when you fell last night. I insisted it be restored, restitched, and cleaned. This is yours, I presume?"

Jab accepted the toy from the imposing rodent. "Thank you. Um, this was my friend's."

Nasalid cocked an eyebrow. "You risked your life to help a friend?" Behind him, the gerbil dressed like a prayer warden smiled and the princely jerboa scoffed.

Kash chuckled. "What else could we expect from the savior of Rattin?"

"Indeed," Nasalid said. "Jab of Rattin, I'm sure Kashdood has informed you that you cannot return home; we must preserve our mission's secrecy. However, I do have something to offer. Kashdood and the other scouts are still learning the area's geography. We need to reclaim ZelZaytun and I will have it done properly. I need a trustworthy local. Your headwraps show you take the All-Planter's words seriously."

Jab gulped. "There's a soldier in your army, a gerbil named Anabeb, who is also from Rattin. Have you asked him to scout?"

Nasalid's whiskers drooped. "That name sounds familiar." He peered at the princely jerboa advisor. "Difatim, where have I read that before?"

Sneering, the jerboa rummaged through a stack of papers. "His name is on the list of casualties."

Had Rijat lied to Mutarra and Qala? Jab couldn't believe his friends' misfortune. He'd had enough of parents being taken away from their children. "He has family who deserves to know." Jab let out a long exhale. This was war. Rodents would die. It was up to the survivors to make sure their sacrifices meant something. "I'll help you take ZelZaytun out of Lady Marjitay's paws."

It's what Sanu would have done.

"Excellent," Nasalid said evenly. He indicated the fourth rodent in the corner, who was a squirrel like Jab and Kash, but had red fur. "I know a camp physician cleared you, but you will also be examined by my personal one, Maimon."

The red squirrel delicately closed his book and rose. "Physician and scientist," he said. "Maimon, at your service." His accent was also unlike anything Jab had ever heard. The princely noble scowled at him. As he rose, decorative twigs knotted into his fur rubbed against each other. This rodent in the tent of Nasalid was a Mulcher.

The Divine Poetics taught that wise and virtuous rodents would seek advice from others with different backgrounds, which is what Nasalid did.

Perhaps this conqueror deserved the title of Liberator. And Jab's aid might reduce unnecessary bloodshed. He could honor Sanu and his own dream.

9

SANU

There are two rodents you must know if you wish to survive on the battlefield: yourself and your enemy.

*- General Ironseed's reprimand
to a failed sergeant*

Entering ZelZaytun to pray had never been Sanu's dream, yet walking inside, hindpaws hitting the same stonework pavement that the heroes of old trod, Sanu appreciated why rodents would fight over this place. Each step either offered cool shade from the olive Gnaverwood or a gentle warmth from a loving sun. A soothing aroma of ginger filled the air, tickling his nostrils and stirring his hunger.

Yet his presence here somehow felt like a betrayal to Jab's memory. His brother wouldn't have wanted anyone to enter this holy place while it was occupied by the Sprouters. And now he stood outside a Sprouter's prayer hall—or whatever they called it—enjoying soothing balms from Freng on his burns, applied by Sprouter healers. He glanced at the salve on his arm. He didn't feel a thing. It was said that Sprouters practiced witchcraft and didn't know the ways of science, yet this cream didn't feel like a fake magic trick. A sniff suggested aloe as an ingredient, which Mom kept at home. Remembering her brought on new pain, a dull throb.

A paw nestled on Sanu's shoulder.

"I'm glad to see you safe inside," Yagub said. "Sir Brouglas was shaking by your bedside all night, worried your burns were beyond the point of recovery. I'll fetch him after he's had some time to rest. Olihort is a true wonder, isn't it?"

"Yeah," Sanu said. "What's that smell?"

Yagub pointed to a bakery across the road. "That is where the olive cakes are made for our Offering Meals. Or maybe you're smelling the sheltercake bakery."

Something tightened in Sanu's stomach. "You ... eat olives?" Sanu never would've cared this much about sacrilege if he weren't trying to honor Jab. No wonder everyone complained the path to the Walled Garden was sealed by these Sprouters. Eating the olives? The All-Planter specifically forbade it. Sanu barely knew anything about his faith, but he did know those were off limits.

Yagub chuckled. "Ah. Yes, I imagine that may come as a surprise. The Sapling would be happy to explain, but Ganan the Gardener, Blest Be Him, told us to enjoy what the All-Planter has provided. It's why we need Olihort. Most Sprouters live on Freng's islands where olives can't grow. A scientist could explain why better than me, but the weather or soil isn't good for them. Eating the sacred olives is part of our faith. If we don't, we can't have the All-Planter within ourselves."

Sanu blinked hard.

As ridiculous as Yagub sounded, his tone was honest. Happy, even.

But was that reason to slaughter the resident Grovekeepers and Mulchers all those years ago? The question formed on Sanu's lips, but if he wanted to be a peacekeeper like Jab, he'd have to swallow it. Yagub and Sir Brouglas had already done so much for him; he couldn't keep insulting them or hold them accountable for something their grandparents may have been ordered to do.

Brouglas was the key. A knight respected enough to have the Sapling's trust might hold enough sway to get to Lady Marjitay's ear. Sprouters and Grovekeepers could share the city somehow.

Sanu also wondered if that idea would make his parents happy. "I think I owe Brouglas some thanks for rescuing me."

Yagub gestured over his shoulder with his thumb. "He's supposed to be resting, but he's back in the Gananhall. He was the only survivor from last night. He's deeply in mourning. He believes the knights' deaths were his fault."

Sir Brouglas didn't deserve all the blame. He didn't know Nasalid had prepared a trap.

Sanu patted his back, and his neck hair stiffened.

"Looking for your scimitar?" Yagub asked. "After Sir Brouglas brought you in, one of Lady Marjitay's retainers asked for it. He said he wished to restore it for you as a favor to Brouglas."

Fighting the urge to shout, Sanu clenched his fists. "Yagub, I need my scimitar back. My dad... It's all I have left of him." An unwelcome tear rose to his eyelid. "Or anyone in my family."

"I see," Yagub replied. "Then I guess you have a reason to enter Olihort's main keep. I would get in trouble if I took you by myself though. Wait here."

While Sanu fumed, he paced around the square. Rodents of every species he'd heard of milled about Olihort, yet not a single one wore the headwraps. Various languages ricocheted between the stone walls. One thing united these Sprouters from the Freng islands—the symbol stitched into their clothing: a rake, the symbol of Ganan the Gardener. Each rake was a different design and size, yet it was always there. While at first Sanu hadn't noticed it on Sir Brouglas' armor, he realized that the center image of Lady Marjitay's banner wasn't a mere line separating the honking goose and crossbow, but also a stylized rake. That was sophisticated art, which was saying something, if Sanu had realized it.

After a few minutes of pacing, Yagub returned with an unarmored Sir Brouglas and a youngish hamster, a teen who looked Qala's age.

Brouglas wrapped Sanu in a powerful hug. "Safe... safe... Praise the All-Planter!"

Yagub muttered something to the beaver knight, who backed away.

The hamster girl introduced herself. "Sanu of Rattin, a pleasure to meet you. I am Cladh. I represent the Sapling of Olihort." Like Qala, Cladh spoke confidently, even though Qawari couldn't have been her first language. Her beige fur had a diamond-shaped patch of white under her chin, and her eyes bore the seriousness of someone who had spent a few too many hours in the classroom.

Sanu waved to her and let out a half chuckle. "It's good to meet you. Can I ask why you're here?"

Cladh held up three fingers. "One, the Sapling wants to know more about Grovekeepers; two, he's busy today; and three, I speak your language better than he does. Three reasons I'm a natural choice." She pointed to an amulet on her necklace: an acorn, dipped in bronze. A green gemstone replaced the acorn's top.

Sanu had imagined storming Lady Marjitay's keep many times, but not quite like this. Yet this was how Jab would do it, and he owed that to his brother.

Perhaps between Sir Brouglas and Yagub, he could learn the languages spoken here and how to swing a sword properly.

10

JAB

Hear, O rodents! I have planted the world itself as much as I have planted all of you. I know each hair on your body as much as I do each grain of sand and blade of grass. Therefore, I know you are all more than the worst thing you have ever done. Share this knowledge.

- *Divine Poetics*

Jab tore his eyes from Rattin's short shadows in the midday sun. Having completed their prayers, it was time for Jab and Kash to depart their perch atop the north horn.

When they reached the bottom of the rocky hill, Jab said, "I saw a jerboa soldier spreading water around the town's perimeter on the side facing ZelZaytun. What was that?"

"Come on, we need to find a place to sketch ZelZaytun. I'll tell you on the way." Kash's tone was grim—the cadence of an older person procrastinating saying something painful.

Kash took off at a jog, and Jab had to run to match his pace. All this running would whip him into shape. Sanu would be proud.

"You saw firstpaw how Nasalid used fire to defeat the Sprouter knights without suffering any of our own casualties, yes?"

Of course Jab had. Just as he saw his brother burn to death. He didn't want to insult Kash or the Liberator though. "Yes."

"Well, we originally thought those knights would go through Rattin and in a larger number. The first plan was to circle the town in fire."

Jab was running too hard to gasp.

After letting the silence hang, Kash continued. "The fire was to cut off their escape. A proper battle would have taken place. But thanks to your information, we were able to meet them between the horns. Nasalid didn't lose a single soldier while taking out a company of knights. You saved lives, Jab. That is why you're the savior of Rattin."

One life wasn't saved.

And Jab shuddered to consider what those knights experienced. Yet Sanu would want Jab to admit that Kash had a point. The knights' heavy armor made them almost invincible against standard weapons, even though it slowed them down.

They reached the halfway point between ZelZaytun and Rattin, not too far from where Jab and Sanu had buried their parents, close to the olive Gnaverwood's shade in the afternoon. Jab doubled over to catch his breath, but Kash stood tall.

"Don't lean over, my friend. Standing straight will let your lungs expand fully. You get more air that way. You'll need every ounce of air for crossbow training later."

Even though it hurt, Jab took the advice. Between breaths, he asked, "Was Nasalid ready to torch the whole town of Rattin?"

Kash's brows furrowed. "It wasn't ideal, but the original belief was that Rattin was a Sprouter depot for colonizers from Freng. I was sent to confirm the information. By the All-Planter's grace, I met you. Jab, war forces rodents to make difficult choices. If it's any consolation, Nasalid has a strict policy against looting. Any soldier caught harming someone who isn't an armed foe is dismissed without pay. Your headwraps display your commitment to the All-Planter's words. I'm sure you've listened to the Divine Poetics all your life. You know the All-Planter does not enjoy violence but does allow defense for the defenseless."

Setting a town aflame was defending the weak, apparently. Jab pushed the sarcasm from his mind. "So why are there soldiers in Rattin now?"

Kash smirked. "They're donating the spoils from last night's victory to the townsrodents. Sprouter weapons and armor are valuable. Their coins spend well too. Other soldiers are spending their own money in the town. It's Nasalid's apology for what he was prepared to do."

Jab sucked in a breath. "Thank you for telling me. Can I show ... you the way to ZelZaytun now? We're nearly there. If it's alright, I'd rather focus on running instead of talking." He couldn't go back into town and show his face. He couldn't bear to see Mutarra and Qala, knowing their dad died.

"Of course," Kash replied. "Let me know if I'm going too fast."

"How about you try ... to keep up?" It's what Sanu would have said. With a deep breath, Jab took off at a sprint toward the holy city, with Kash keeping pace at his side. Shamefully, Jab realized Kash wasn't exerting himself much. Jab was excited by the prospect that he might get to run as fast as Kash one day, even burdened with a crossbow.

They ran until they arrived at a grassy bank overlooking the outer stone gate to the city. His hindpaws throbbed, commiserating and congratulating in equal measure. Jab took an angle where he could gaze upon the city without having to avert his eyes from the olive Gnaverwood, and Kash followed suit.

Kash marveled at the sight. "You know, when it's just a dot in the distance, Nasalid's holy men tell us we don't need to avert our eyes, since it could be an illusion or mirage from such a distance. But here, seeing its shadow, I can feel its holy presence. Thank you for showing this to me, Jab. You're positive this was the fastest route?"

"Fastest for us on hindpaw. I don't know how an army on horseback would do."

"That's a problem for the officers." Kash crouched and pulled a wad of paper and nub of charcoal from his knapsack. He unfolded and stretched the paper over the grass.

"Are you sketching a map?" Jab asked. Sanu would want to smack him for asking such an obvious question. He might as well have asked what the crossbow was for.

"Yes, and making notes. Say, do you happen to know what kind of stone they used for the walls?"

"The walls?" How could Jab possibly know? "I'm sorry, Kash. I think you might need to ask a scientist to identify them for you."

Kash glanced up from his sketch and shot Jab an apologetic smile and a playful tsk. "I'm not a scientist and I'm interested in minerals and architecture. Anyway, that's the outer wall built by the Sprouters after they stole the city, right?"

Jab nodded. "That's about all I know."

"Did your parents ever mention if the stone was local or imported from one of the Freng islands? That could give me a clue."

"Imported," Jab whispered. Memories surfaced of Mom and Dad laughing with Rijat about how the Sprouters would've bankrupted themselves by funding the wall. They'd called it something only a boring adult would find funny. "Lady Marjitay's purse," as if she built the wall herself or funded it with anything other than oppressive taxes.

"Knowing the color, size, and possible origin of the stone will suffice for the engineers." He rose and pocketed his charcoal. "Jab, I have to look at the Gnaverwood. I need to sketch everything's relative height. If I'm wrong, my mistakes could lead to a catapult firing on the Gnaverwood."

Jab reminded himself Kash wasn't committing sacrilege, just ignoring a popular practice since ZelZaytun's fall. Jab turned around to avoid watching Kash experience the ecstasy of gazing upon the holy tree for the first time.

"By the All-Planter," Kash gasped. "It's magnificent."

A single tear welled in Jab's eye. Every Grovekeeper deserved to see it. But only in its true splendor: after the Sprouters' evil was purged.

"Is this where Nasalid will attack ZelZaytun?"

"We need to see the entire perimeter to help the Liberator make that judgment call. I know he'll want to strike wherever there are the fewest civilians and holy buildings. But I don't know what his advisors will think. It's not our place to tell him where to go, only to make suggestions."

Jab glanced at the map sketch—sloppier than he would have guessed. "Then let me show you the rest of the city walls and maybe you can keep drawing."

Siege tactics.

The business was deplorable. If one piece of bark chipped off the olive Gnaverwood, perhaps the way to the Walled Garden would never reopen, and his parents would be doomed. Everyone would be.

11

SANU

Each step in ZelZaytun filled Sanu with a sense of history he never would've appreciated by reading. Even though he didn't believe the Sprouters' Ganan the Gardener was a miracle worker and the All-Planter's final messenger, he still respected him as a moral teacher, even without Jab's religious knowledge. Sanu knew Ganan said to treat everyone kindly. Jab once said so, quoting from that book by some philosopher named Rattyshenna or something.

And this was the city where Ganan preached hundreds of years ago. Ancient Mulcher kings resided here, building the first original grove fence around the sacred Gnaverwood in the time before Sprouterism and Grovekeeping became the dominant faiths. Mulchers still lived here until the Sprouters slaughtered those who wouldn't convert. The idea sent a shiver up Sanu's spine. This place was coated in history, faith, and blood. And if the Sprouters wouldn't share or vacate the city, more blood would follow at Nasalid's paws.

Weren't religions supposed to be peaceful?

Yet the Sprouters living here seemed happy. Smiling porcupines, beavers, and squirrels—both brown and gray—all saluted and waved. The greetings Sir Brouglas received were more jovial, with friendly tail taps, and Cladh's were more reverent, with bowed heads, especially after spying her amulet. Yagub and Sanu got a few, but they were afterthoughts following the knight and representative of the Sapling. The citizens' politeness didn't change the fact that their grandparents took this city from others.

They passed the shrines of Mulchers which had been converted into other buildings, and the Grovekeeper prayer halls—once great feats of architecture—into storehouses for weapons and barracks for soldiers. Jab would call that a disgrace or something, but Sanu found the weapons fascinating.

Yagub caught Sanu staring at a converted prayer hall and nudged him. "Not all Sprouters are happy about how the Grovekeeper buildings have been treated."

Cladh tutted. "If it weren't for Lady Marjitay's family and ancestors, things would be much different around here."

Brouglas slapped the stone street with his tail to catch her attention. He muttered something to her in Frenglese.

Yagub translated for Sanu. "Not everyone agrees with us and the Sapling about Lady Marjitay's leadership or that of her late father and grandfather. We must be careful." He nodded and waved to an armed porcupine guard standing watch before a stone door.

Sanu gazed at the building's height and Yagub explained. "This was King's Keep, built by the legendary second Mulcher king of ZelZaytun, Suleimouse—one of the many rodents revered and respected by Grovekeeper, Mulcher, and Sprouter."

Sir Brouglas greeted the guard, who eyed Sanu.

Cladh stepped forward, and after saying something boisterous, displayed her amulet, a gold-dipped acorn with a gemstone replacing the top. With a reverent nod, the guard stepped aside. His armor, modified for his quills, bore Lady Marjitay's symbol in brighter colors than those on Sir Brouglas' armor. In that moment, Sanu wondered if the beaver knight allowed Marjitay's insignia to fade on purpose so he could get in better with Rattin's townsrodents. Or maybe he'd let them fade because he wasn't enthusiastic about her leadership. His heart lightened at the possibility but sank harder realizing Nasalid burned the like-minded rodents alive at Rattin.

Passing the guard, Sanu ogled this rodent's weapon: an impressive polearm, sporting the characteristics of a pike and a hammer, resembling a weaponized crow's beak from the Droughtlands. This beast of a spear-hammer hybrid could probably perforate or snap the heaviest steel armor and look awesome in the process. Sanu wouldn't say that he wanted one, but he definitely needed one.

When they entered the keep, mosaics spread across the walls and ceiling. Yagub pointed up at them. "These depict scenes from the Mulchers' mythology, revered as fact by some and appreciated as metaphor by others."

Jab would want to know more and Dad would've loved to stop and admire each image. Sanu tugged on Yagub's elbow. "Ask Sir Brouglas if he knows what that porcupine's weapon is and if he can teach me to use it."

"It's called a devilbeak," Cladh said. "I saw you drool over it. Don't get offended, but you're too small."

"She's right," Yagub agreed.

Brouglas tapped the floor with his tail to get their attention and said a short phrase. He pointed to where another armed beaver saluted him, and they followed him down the stone hall.

Sanu blinked hard, realizing he understood what Brouglas had said. "This way." Learning a language would be as useful as swinging a sword properly. But mastering the Devilbeak would still be cooler.

Navigating these halls felt like a lesson in history and culture. The walls preserved the oldest

Mulcher artwork, meaning both Grovekeeper and Sprouter appreciated it, or at least didn't find it offensive. The sharper, carved lines in the ceiling were the work of Grovekeeper architects, for improving the structural integrity.

The Sprouter leaders either didn't know this was Grovekeeper design or respected the functionality. Stained glass windows replaced what was once open windows with no covering. That had to be from the Sprouters, not only because of the foreign art style, but also because they came from a much colder climate and needed true windows.

"The whole complex is several floors, but we don't need to climb any stairs," Yagub said as they passed a spiraling staircase. "Those all lead to the living quarters. The tradition since the Mulcher kings has been to do all legal and political business on the first floor."

On their left, open double doors revealed a dining hall big enough to fit every rodent in Rattin, and maybe a few of their cousins.

Sanu wondered how much gold was spent on this complex through the years, and if Lady Marjitay saw herself as part of the line of the ancient Mulcher kings. Ironic, considering her grandfather killed their descendants and she called herself a Sprouter Queen.

Ahead, two larger double doors loomed, guarded by two armored squirrels. Their armor was much more stylized, decorated with plumage and ribbons. Their gripped devilbeaks showed they could still fight and defend, but they'd never last on a battlefield without tripping over their ornamentation.

Sir Brouglas saluted them, and they returned the gesture. He said something, and Sanu realized he figured out which sounds meant "Lady Marjitay." He'd need to check with Yagub, but he was pretty sure Brouglas said that they were here to see the lady of the castle. Brouglas gestured to Cladh, who displayed her amulet again.

The pair of armored squirrels nodded, rotated to face each other, and pulled the doors open, revealing the throne room, which Sprouters believed was a representation of the All-Planter's court on Pruning Day. Sanu was worried Lady Marjitay would "prune" him in here. And occupying it was a mole rat, not seated upon the throne, but posing for a portrait artist. She held a crossbow too ornate to be used in combat, and she definitely had the wrong posture for effective wielding.

An energetic porcupine attendant rushed up to their group and spoke.

Yagub translated. "She said Lady Marjitay will be having a break soon from getting her portrait painted." With a sigh, he added, "And that we should be honored to be in her good presence."

Brouglas stared at his hindpaws.

Cladh scoffed. "And she also told us that Lady Marjitay has invited us to wait in the dining hall, where we can eat at a discounted rate."

"Some host," Sanu mumbled.

Posing with her crossbow, Lady Marjitay's flowing green gown displayed her family coat of arms with a honking goose and another crossbow.

"Yagub," Sanu whispered. "What's with her and all the crossbows?"

The older squirrel sighed. "Some Sprouter nobles believe the common rodent likes crossbows. They want to distinguish themselves as in league with the commoners for their continued support. They think showing off their crossbows will accomplish that."

Sanu's eyes widened. "Could an average Sprouter afford a weapon like that back on your home islands?" He knew Nasalid's scouts carried smaller crossbows, but what she held looked more like a heavy decoration than an actual weapon.

"Of course not," Cladh said. "Not with the way nobles like her tax them and spend the money on themselves."

Sir Brouglas shook his head and pointed at Cladh's amulet. He snarled something at the porcupine attendant, who backed off.

"He told her that the Sapling's request cannot be denied for a non-emergency," Yagub translated. "That she is not above the All-Planter's will."

Sanu nodded and noticed the throne guards glowering at Brouglas.

The porcupine made a hasty curtsy before jogging to the posing mole rat.

Lady Marjitay threw down her crossbow and squeaked something at the poor artist. She said something else, and her shrill voice spiked through the art-covered room.

Sanu understood what she said, which made his fur stand on end, because almost without realizing it, he obeyed, finding himself approaching her.

The other three also came forward, necks and chins stiff.

Cladh and Brouglas took turns explaining to her what happened at the horns of Rattin and the Sapling's opinion on it.

Yagub translated as much as he could, but the hamster, beaver, and mole rat were exchanging verbal barbs too fast. "The lady has suggested Brouglas is a coward for escaping the battle. Cladh defended him, and she is none too pleased that you are here. She is giving Sir Brouglas a mission away from Olihort." Yagub's voice dropped as he translated the next exchange. "She plans to empty the other forts to prepare for Nasalid's attack here."

"How does she know Nasalid will attack?"

"Because we saw Nasalid's banner outside Rattin. He is amassing forces and already wiped out a company of knights. Olihort's defenses are weak."

"What if she surrendered to Nasalid?"

And there it was: he'd said the most hated word. Surrender.

Yagub stared at him. Cladh glanced back too.

"What did he say?" Lady Marjitay squeaked in Frenglese, and Sanu understood her.

Cladh's whiskers stiffened, and she pivoted to wave a finger at Lady Marjitay. She translated, and Sanu became confident he knew their word for "surrender" now.

Sanu summoned courage to try his first sentence in their language. "Surrender to Nasalid."

Lady Marjitay pointed at her crossbow and glared at him, muttering something.

"S-she said to watch your tongue," Yagub translated, "or she'll cut it out."

All eyes in the room fixated on Sanu as he felt the blood draining from his face. "Yagub, can you explain that Nasalid is a virtuous liberator? If she surrendered peacefully, Nasalid would let everyone here live, or at least leave in peace."

Yagub scratched the back of his head. "I don't think anyone will believe me."

Cladh waved a paw. "Sanu is right. Nasalid's honor is legendary. Rodents talk about him across the sea, even in Freng."

Lady Marjitay squealed and grabbed her crossbow off the floor. She said something that sounded generally horrific, and her expression rattled Sanu's bones.

She pointed the lethal weapon at Yagub and motioned for him to translate.

"She said if we mention his name again or discuss surrendering, we'll be executed."

No wonder Brouglas resented her. She resembled the Sprouters in fairy tales and stories. She probably didn't eat children, but it wouldn't be a surprising detail to discover. She shifted her aim to Sanu, and he stared down the loaded crossbow, as she muttered something in Frenglese.

He didn't want a translation.

12

JAB

The All-Planter does hear and respond to all prayers. Remember that "No" is a legitimate response, and sometimes a more loving one. What loving parent would say yes when their child asked to play with fire or a viper? As a parent knows much more than a child, how much more does the All-Planter know than you?

- Raticenna's collected sermons

Not too far away from where he'd buried his parents, Jab examined as much of ZelZaytun as possible without gazing upon the sacred olive Gnaverwood. Temptation bubbled to pester Kash with questions about the sight, but he forced it down. Knowing his parents and brother would never look upon it brought up a feeling in Jab he didn't understand.

"We have one more piece of business." Kash's voice carried the slightest tremor as he found himself overcome with emotion from the sight of the holy tree.

"What is it?" Hearing Kash's ecstasy made him want to be more positive.

Even though these military matters were Sanu's dream, living it for his brother was exhilarating in a way Jab hadn't expected, almost as if Sanu were still alive. And scouting was innocent. Unless they screwed up their crossbow training, nobody died because of scouts.

A tremor ran through his conscience as he finished the thought. Those Sprouter knights died because of what Jab told Kash. Yet the rodents of Rattin may have died because of a bad report from another scout, and they were all innocent. This was war, and rodents would die on both sides. Jab vowed to minimize the suffering and carnage as much as possible.

"We're missing a Sprouter depot. Since we can rule out Rattin, an outpost somewhere nearby must be supplying ZelZaytun. It's too far removed from the coast where the Sprouter's castles and forts are. There has to be some way-point between here and the ports."

"So if it's not Rattin, have you tried the other side of the road leading into ZelZaytun?" Jab asked.

"That's our next destination. We have to take the roundabout way, though, I'm afraid."

"So we won't get seen?"

"So we're less likely to be seen. Some things are unavoidable. I have coin to buy silence and a dagger to ensure it." His tone was as dark as the reality that he wasn't much older than Qala and was ready to kill someone for a secret.

Jab shivered. "Maybe we could say we're shepherds or hunters or something if anyone bumps into us."

"I've used worse alibis. Come on, keep your eye on the road in the distance."

The two squirrels crossed the jagged grass fields, passing droning goats and a hawk tearing apart a viper.

Perhaps Nasalid would be the hawk tearing apart the snakes in ZelZaytun. Jab pushed the idea from his mind. Sprouters were still rodents, even if they'd done horrific things.

Keeping up with Kash became increasingly difficult as they rounded the holy city. Kash leapt over rocks without breaking his stride, and Jab wondered if he could outrun a horse.

None of this was to mention the extra gear Kash carried. He ran with cooking implements, both their bedrolls, his sketching supplies, and a light crossbow on his hip—not the large monstrosities Sprouters used, but one meant for fast loading.

Clouds passed overhead, marching about the sky. Jab wondered what the clouds did upon contact with the Gnaverwood. Maybe they respectfully went around, or bumped into the tree, oblivious as they were. Drinking clouds would be an interesting way for the tree to get moisture and sustenance. Although he wasn't sure if a Gnaverwood would need any sustenance in the first place.

When they arrived at a patch of cedar trees, Jab begged Kash to stop. Propping himself against a trunk, he wheezed for air. "I'm sorry," he said between gasps. "I don't want to disappoint Nasalid and make you late."

"Don't be," Kash soothed. "I'm impressed you kept up. It's nice doing this with someone." He undid his pack and tossed Jab his water flask. "Drink slow. Don't worry about the Liberator. He'd rather have a thorough report than a rushed one. Besides, part of this mission involves training the newest recruit, the savior of Rattin. It's an honor for me."

"Savior of Rattin" burned Jab's ears. The title wouldn't bring Sanu back.

After a few timid sips, he returned the flask to Kash. "Thank you. I'm—"

Honk-honk!

Jab stumbled, looking for the source of the sound.

Hiss!

"Ha!" Kash exclaimed. "A goose!"

Jab whipped around. A white-gray goose approached them, wings outstretched. Brown patches circled its eyes like war paint.

"One of the meanest creatures made by the All-Planter," Jab muttered.

"I should re-introduce you to Difatim and Jorjim if you think that's true."

Jab grabbed a rock by his hindpaws; he didn't want to hurt the bird, just get it to leave.

Kash rested his tail on Jab's wrist. "Don't. He's defending his territory."

"How can you tell it's a boy?" Jab dropped his rock, letting it roll by his hindpaws.

"Vibrant feathers. Boy birds almost always have the prettier feathers. It's how they impress the ladies."

The goose hissed again, and Jab accidentally let his cynical side out. "That's much easier than fighting wars."

"I can tell you with confidence I have never impressed a lady." Kash smirked. "Back away slowly. He's protecting some goslings."

Behind the defiant bird, some fluffy-feathered babies stumbled around, weakly honking in imitation of their father. He wished he could show Mutarra; she'd love to fawn over them.

The goslings cleared the path behind their father, bumping into each other all the way to a bush. Once they passed, the father goose lowered his wings but kept his menacing goose gaze fixed on them, more threatening than a dragon from a fairy tale.

"This was a good find," Kash said.

"What do you mean?"

"Junior scout, use some inductive reasoning. If we found geese, what must be close?"

"Water?"

"What kind?"

They weren't anywhere near the Great Sea. "Fresh water."

"Do you know if there's a lake or river nearby?" Kash asked.

"There's a freshwater lake somewhere around ZelZaytun," Jab said. "But my parents never let any of the kids in our town come out this far."

"All that matters is we're close." Kash smiled the way Dad would while teaching Sanu and Jab something. "Now, we aren't too far off from sunset. So do you think the geese were going to or from the water?"

"From. How do you know so much about birds?"

Kash followed the goose tracks. Their wet feet had patted down an obvious path for them, even though the ground wasn't too muddy. "I'm in nature all the time," Kash said. "You saw how awkward I am around rodents, especially strangers."

Jab clicked his tongue. "Birds make more sense to you than rodents?" Kash *had* been a bit weird during their first meeting.

"They get to fly free. They aren't chained by responsibilities and politics. Not having to train with crossbows must be nice too. I think that's why Nasalid likes falconry."

They pressed between closely-packed cedars and shrubs.

"But birds don't know the All-Planter like we do." Jab tried not to scoff at the older squirrel. How could he be jealous of a dumb animal?

"What if the opposite is true, Jab?" Kash pulled a shrub branch away so Jab could pass. "What if the All-Planter only revealed the Divine Poetics to rodents because we are the ones who are lost? Plants and animals do exactly what they're supposed to do. We're the ones who steal and murder."

The ground underneath them softened.

Jab sighed. The possibility of a goose being closer to the All-Planter's will than he was stung, but also made a type of sense. If anything, it was an invitation to be more compassionate toward lower animals. Maybe he should stop calling them lower animals too. They couldn't think or talk like rodents, but the All-Planter still loved them.

Kash turned and gently grabbed Jab's shoulders. "Focus on listening. What do you hear?"

Jab's ears perked. "Water!"

Smiling, Kash pulled aside another branch, revealing a lake rimmed by cedars. "Now keep your voice down. What do you see on the water?"

Jab squinted until he found a trio of fishing boats. On the opposite shore, several squat buildings formed a semicircle around a dock. In the middle of them stood a slightly taller stone structure with the unmistakable symbol of the Sprouters' rake. Two banners fluttered in the gentle breeze. Straining his eyes, Jab noticed the faint image on them: goose and crossbow.

"This is the supply station," Jab whispered. "They're bringing extra fish into ZelZaytun from here."

"Excellent work, scout," Kash said. "Let's make some sketches and return to camp."

13

SANU

*- General Ironseed's second letter
to the Five Princes of Qawar*

A sword raced toward Sanu's head. He dodged it, losing some ear hair in the process.

The barracks' training pit stored all the weapons racks and dummies Sanu had ever hoped for.

"Good!" Sir Brouglas said, using a new word Sanu learned in their language, Frenglese. The beaver smiled and said something Sanu intuited meant, "Your turn." Frenglese was getting easier to understand as he spent more time there.

He lifted his longsword, a loan from the beaver knight. It was heavier than Dad's scimitar—currently unavailable since one of Lady Marjitay's other knights insisted on paying to have it restored, which was nice but also unsettling, and Sanu couldn't explain why.

Scimitar design demanded slashes, but this blade's shape called for thrusts. Sanu stabbed at a different angle to accommodate for their different heights.

With an armored sleeve, Sir Brouglas caught Sanu's attack in the crook of his elbow, then pulled Sanu down. Laughing, Sanu dropped the weapon and crumpled to the sandy pit.

Yagub called from the other side of the fence. "I don't recommend trying that block without armor."

Sanu wanted to reply that he wasn't dumb, but he thanked the older squirrel for the tip. He was only offering advice, and Sanu wasn't wearing armor.

Behind them, the gate partitioning the military quarter from the housing district raised with a series of clanks. Cladh left the gatehouse and plodded beside Yagub. "Sorry to end the session, but Sir Brouglas has been summoned by the Sapling." She repeated the news in Frenglese to Brouglas. The beaver knight flipped his sword and offered the hilt to Sanu. "Try ... with ... two. Fun."

Yagub groaned. "For the love of the Gardener, do not try with two, Sanu! You'll chop your whiskers off."

Sanu tried a technique he'd practiced earlier, twirling both swords at the same time. He didn't cut his whiskers, but he did nearly smack himself.

Flourishing stunts with weapons would get him hurt if he botched them or wasted precious energy before a fight. He was pretty sure there was a warrior maxim about discretion and good judgment in battle.

Another voice slowly approached, allowing Sanu to catch the words, "I," "train," and "boy." The speaker was a porcupine knight Sanu had seen on their earlier tour of the sacred city's palace. He then switched languages, and his pronunciation of Qawari was flawless. "Sanu, I saw you eyeing the devilbeak earlier when you visited the palace."

A younger squirrel ran up behind him, holding the coolest piece of steel Sanu had ever laid eyes on. The porcupine knight accepted it from the squirrel, then rotated, revealing Sanu's scimitar on his waist. "I brought this back to you. I insisted that Lady Marjitay's best blacksmith restore it." The knight opened the fence and stepped inside the training sand.

"T-thank you," Sanu stuttered. "Sir..."

"Sir Zantiz," he finished. He turned to the others. Sanu thought he said something about the two of them being fine, and to give the Sapling something. He guessed it was his regards or greeting.

Yagub, Cladh and Sir Brouglas waved to Sanu and headed toward the Gananhall.

With a disarming smile, Sir Zantiz passed the scimitar to Sanu, then wielded the devilbeak in both paws. "Take some practice cuts. Away from me, please." He laughed.

Sanu swung. No more notches or scuffs. Yet it was still Dad's. Jab would have been happy, knowing this built a relationship with the enemy. The former enemy.

"It's perfect, Sir Zantiz. Tell the blacksmith I'm in his debt."

"No need, Sanu. He and I were happy to behold fine craftwork. It's such a beautiful design and it was a pleasure to examine it closely. Like Sir Brouglas and our beloved Sapling, I'm interested in learning about our Grovekeeper neighbors. I thought perhaps you could be my teacher. And in exchange, I'll teach you to fight with a proper weapon."

Sanu's eyes widened. This couldn't be real.

"I saw your thrust with a longsword. Show me a diagonal slash with your blade."

Sanu complied.

"Your shoulder and arm were in the right position, but the power comes from your hip. Try again."

Sanu followed the suggestion, and the scimitar *whished* through the air.

"Excellent. Now cut at me, half speed, please. While we train, please indulge my curiosity. I learned Grovekeepers pray throughout the day. Are the times set?"

The blade connected with the devilbeak's shaft. If Sanu had been going at full speed or Sir Zantiz used a more aggressive posture, Sanu would have bounced right off, or worse, the sword would've lodged in the wood without breaking it.

Sanu followed the reverberations in his arm as the blade bounced away from the attack. "There are prayers at the major solar changes throughout the day. Sunrise, noon, and sunset."

"Interesting. Try that attack again from the opposite direction. What else can you tell me?"

Sanu swung, and he would've pulled a muscle if he were going full strength. This angle and force were unkind to his elbow. He'd be sore tomorrow. "Uh, some rodents, like my brother, will pray more. Like midmorning and midday."

"Our ritual service—an Offering Meal—lasts an hour on most days. How long does yours take?" A hunger ran underneath Sir Zantiz's words.

"A few minutes—longer if you walk to the prayer house first, but not everyone does."

Zantiz shifted his stance for Sanu's next strike. "And you must stop whatever you're doing to pray?"

"Well, I guess if there's an emergency or something, we wouldn't stop," Sanu half-chuckled. Jab would've liked this kind of back-and-forth.

Sir Zantiz's eyes showed a flicker of disappointment, and he switched his grip on the devilbeak. "Now, try to block an incoming attack. I'll go slowly." He began his demonstration with a thrust. The devilbeak boasted a sharp point crosswise to its conical tip and a hammer end. Three weapons in one: swinging hammer, culling hook, and skewering spearpoint.

Zantiz wielded it like a spear and attacked. Sanu slashed to push it away. In the space of a blink, the porcupine knight twisted the devil-beak, catching Sanu's scimitar between the hook and spearpoint.

Sanu's grip on his sword fumbled. "That's a cool move." Fearful reverence rocked his voice. At full speed with direct contact, this would have punctured Sanu's organs.

"I'll repeat the motion; see if you can escape the hold. Now, I've heard that during the summer, Grovekeepers won't eat during daylight. Is that true?"

"It's the month after the winter solstice. My brother told me this reminds the wealthy to be compassionate for rodents who experience homelessness and poverty."

Sir Zantiz thrust the spear, Sanu slashed, and the blade capture maneuver overwhelmed Sanu again. "Try wiggling your blade the opposite direction. You know, Sprouters fast too. It's a somber time of year. Yours must be too."

Sanu grunted against Zantiz's lock—the porcupine was stronger than the grays around his muzzle suggested. "Our fasting time isn't sad. We have a nice party at dinner, because it's like everyone won a competition." Dad had joked that he loved the fasting time because skipping a meal saved food money. Both Sanu and Jab enjoyed fasting since it combined faith and a toughness challenge.

Sanu wriggled the blade, felt a slight give, then Sir Zantiz laid down more pressure and Sanu was stuck again. "I don't know how to get out. Am I too weak?"

Zantiz twisted the devilbeak and let Sanu step back. "Too weak *now*. You'll build strength this way."

Sanu smiled, hoping this training session would never end.

"Is fasting mandatory? Try blocking a hammer strike now." Zantiz rotated the devilbeak. "All the men fast? No exceptions?" The porcupine knight swung again, faster.

Sanu slashed up to catch and deflect it. "The warden told my neighbor not to after he got sick. But yeah, everyone does this. It's coming up soon."

Zantiz's gaze remained fixed on Sanu's scimitar, as if doing some math about the angle of the strike. A grin curled up the porcupine's snout. "Excellent. You seem tired, young Sanu. Let's join your companions."

Catching his breath, Sanu thanked him, wondering why Zantiz was so curious.

14

JAB

Hear, O rodents! The difference between your richest and your poorest displeases me. If you want access to the Walled Garden, let your society imitate it. Widows, those experiencing homelessness, and orphans all must receive donations. The stingier you are in your donations, the harsher you can expect my judgment to be on Pruning Day.

- Divine Poetics

The days after the discovery of the lake depot involved so much crossbow training, Jab heard the crank's *racka-click* in his sleep. While Nasalid's troops prepared for a raid, Jab practiced shooting targets. Running toward them and firing, running away from them and firing, and worst of all, loading and running at the same time.

But different running happened today.

Fresh from their sunset prayers, mounted archers, riders with unlit torches, and lightly armored soldiers with clubs splintered apart from their formation, circling around the lake.

Jab bounced on the saddle while Kash directed his horse, Macarona, through the trees. Macarona's coal-colored coat matched the darkening night around them. She'd taken a liking to Jab after he offered her a pomegranate intended for target practice. She seemed unbothered by her riders' combined weight, possibly because she smelled the extra fruit Jab had in his scout's pouch.

Nasalid, his top two advisors, and his top lieutenants rode to the right. Kash and Jab had been afforded the privilege to ride alongside Nasalid's war council on the journey to the raid, despite Difatim's protest. The princely jerboa advisor, Difatim, didn't take kindly to Nasalid's methods, which made Jab wonder why he was there in the first place.

The mounted archers and torchbearers emerged from the grass and occupied the road, blocking any escape to ZelZaytun, while the infantry spread through the trees which concealed the lake.

Tonight's attack on the supply station would weaken the Sprouters before Nasalid's siege of ZelZaytun. The siege would be quicker, and Jab would have prevented at least some deaths.

Once in formation, Nasalid summoned Kash and Jab with a wave, along with his lieutenant.

His voice was stern, yet barely a whisper. "Their tallest building is a Gananshed. If it's unoccupied, send in one unarmed soldier to verify. If there's a seedling, or any rodent who has taken their holy vows, bring them to me unharmed. There will be gold in there. It shall remain. Whoever loots will be sent home empty pawed. If any rodent refuses to accept a surrender, he will be sent home unpaid."

The lieutenant, Jorjim, and Difatim scowled at the Liberator, both jerboas twitching their wide ears.

"Am I clear?" Nasalid persisted.

"Yes, Liberator," the lieutenant mumbled. The burly jerboa scowled at the two squirrels.

Nasalid turned to Kash. "Ensure Difatim gives my message true. Relay updates back to me as the attack progresses."

"Understood," Kash replied.

Jab knew it wasn't his place to speak. For the number of troops who had journeyed here, Jab couldn't believe the quiet. Barely a rodent spoke.

Astride Macarona, Kash and Jab trailed lieutenant Jorjim, who had affixed a club to his tail. Jorjim had the ferocity of a warrior spirit in him, and his muscles and scars proved the jerboa climbed the army's ranks from battle prowess, not some fancy education like some of Nasalid's other higher-ups. His grim brutality was an odd symmetry to Nasalid's dour nobility. Both were severe: one in word, the other in action. Jorjim had certainly earned the extra falcon feathers in his helmet.

They navigated through the trees, and Jab observed the boats bobbing alongside the dock.

Lamplight spilled from the few buildings surrounding the lake, most of which was coming from the tallest building. The workers, or soldiers, or whoever lived here would be turning in for sleep soon.

Leaning around Macarona's neck and head, Jab noticed a white oval of feathers plodding into the path.

An adult goose, maybe the same one from last week.

Wordless, Jorjim rode up to it and bashed it with his tail club. The mess of feathers fell—the poor creature didn't have time to squawk or honk.

Jab gasped, and Kash released one paw from Macarona's reins to mute him. "Shh. One stray noise could betray our position. Be glad this wasn't a Sprouter lookout." Already whispering, Kash dropped his voice even lower. "Here's your first glimpse of death on the battlefield, but don't expect the next one to be easier to manage."

Jab tensed. He didn't want to see anything die, even a lower animal, and definitely not another rodent.

Passing the bloodied feathers, Jab muttered a prayer on the bird's behalf, for a father trying to protect his kids.

Maybe that's what happened with his grandparents. They'd died to let their kids escape.

He heard a rustle of leaves in a nearby bush.

Two tiny eyes over a goose beak poked out. Jab stared into Macarona's mane and said a prayer for the goslings too.

Kash brought Macarona to a halt as Jorjim commanded the sergeants, who would relay the order to their squads. Jab didn't completely understand how the army was organized yet, but knew Jorjim's extra feathers on his helmet meant a greater rank.

Jab's heart raced—he was a piece of this structure now. Which was unfortunate, since he'd blanked out while Jorjim conveyed Nasalid's orders.

The sergeants' expressions ran the gamut from dour to excited.

Night raids weren't noble—this would bring no glory, just as the fire attack against the band of Sprouter knights wasn't noble. Fiery slaughter couldn't have been what Sanu wanted. It certainly wasn't what Jab wanted.

Yet the fire on Rattin's horns, and this raid would save lives, although Jab wasn't sure if the benefit outweighed the price.

Packs of three, five, and seven soldiers emerged from the trees, and slunk through the station, while others cut off exits and clearer paths away from the main road.

No Sprouters would escape. Those who survived this confrontation would be taken prisoner.

Two of Nasalid's patrollers trotted between the trees, effortless and graceful on horseback, watching for stragglers or other routes of escape, and providing backup if needed.

The infantry encircled, then descended, clubbing open locked doors. Thuds and yelps reverberated through the still night. Jab tensed, feeling the weight of his light crossbow. Rodents were getting killed mere yards away from him. The same buildings he watched now had dead bodies in them. The tall building with the rake symbol soon had a Sprouter standing atop it, still in nightclothes.

He shouted something in Frenglese, and the noise reverberated through the area.

A quartet of Sprouter knights, fully armored, emerged from the Gananshed. Their plate mail caught and reflected the gentle moonlight, turning it into a fierce glow. They brandished weapons unlike anything Jab had seen before: long polearms boasting a center spear, a hammer, and a curved spike.

Two packs of three soldiers charged them, but these knights stood their ground. The two center knights, both porcupines, stabbed into their targets, and Nasalid's attackers fell. Meanwhile, the two flanking knights swiped the hooked sides of their weapons, pulling two other attackers down and pinning them in place. One soldier pulled back, swapped his club for a bow and arrow, and loosed a projectile, which bounced harmlessly off them. The final soldier feinted left, then bashed the polearm itself with his club.

Jab winced at the squelch, crunch, and screams of Nasalid's fallen soldiers. They were killed thoughtlessly, like the goose. He remembered the fiery battle that killed Sanu, who was as innocent and harmless as the goose. Shivering in the heat of battle, Jab wondered if he'd be next.

Each of these four knights wore heavy plate mail which enclosed their bodies. Their helmets had mere slits for eyes and holes for air, concealing their species. They looked like something from an apocalyptic nightmare—enemies of the All-Planter, more monster than rodent.

A swarm of Nasalid's soldiers bravely descended on them with clubs and maces, bashing the metal armor until it dented. The metal clangs shook Jab's eardrums.

The fray went from the four knights brutally defending each other to a pile of writhing bodies.

"The battle is won," Kash whispered. "We need to report back to Nasalid."

A cheer rang out from behind them, and doors creaked open with captured Sprouters leaving the buildings.

Jab couldn't look back to see the dead.

What would Sanu say? "Kash, why were the infantry using clubs? Isn't that a primitive weapon?"

"Clubs and maces," Kash corrected.

Jab couldn't believe himself asking such a ridiculous question after witnessing people die in front of him. But knowing Sanu would've been curious helped.

Oblivious to Jab's inner pain, Kash continued. "Scimitars are phenomenal weapons against a mounted soldier. Blades to stab or slash were not meant for metal armor. The Sprouter knights are almost impervious to damage in them. But a club, mace, or hammer can crush armor, or crush the rodent inside it. Internal injuries. Something the legendary General Ironseed figured out, unfortunately, too late. The other way to beat these armored knights is exhaustion, especially in the sunlight on a hot day. It's why our main force is mounted archers who engage to invite a false charge, then a fast retreat to tire them out. It's also why we are cutting off this station. We're denying them fresh water and fish."

Jab shuddered. "Nasalid wants to defeat the Sprouter army by dehydrating them?" Somehow, getting cut down quickly in a battle seemed more civilized. At least that would end fast.

"He could find someone to invent a better sword, spear, or arrow to penetrate their thick armor, which would still endanger Grovekeepers, or he can beat them creatively and save lives. Using heavy crossbows like Sprouters do would slow everyone down and rob us of our primary advantage. Which would you prefer?" Kash's tone sounded like a kind teacher losing patience.

Even Macarona looked back at Jab after that.

Jab exhaled, doing everything in his power to push the echo of screaming from his mind.

15

SANU

Sanu pulled the tunic over his head, examining the fit. It itched worse than Dad's old clothes. Sir Brouglas had requested Sanu get strictly plain clothes, but they couldn't find any his size.

Sanu, sitting on a bed in the basement of a Sprouter Gananhall, wore clothes provided to him by Sir Zantiz. Sporting Lady Marjitay's coat of arms meant he was also wearing a giant rake symbol. Although he preferred a rake to the goose and crossbow, the insult of wearing the symbol of his people's oppressor *and* her religion stung. Yet Sir Zantiz assured him Sanu's clothes would be clean tomorrow.

Sanu slumped from the room, grabbing his restored scimitar with sore arms and calloused fingers. The last week had been little else but training with Zantiz and Brouglas, answering their questions about Grovekeepers and building up his skills in speaking Frenglese.

"Don't look *too* happy," Cladh said. She thumbed the Sapling's amulet around her neck. The bronze-dipped acorn echoed the gleam of her eyes.

He blinked hard, realizing he was staring at her instead of responding. "Oh, um. Yeah, I ... don't really like wearing Ganan's rake."

Cladh pointed toward the stairs. "I would've been more upset wearing Lady Marjitay's banner. I thought Grovekeepers respected Ganan, Blest Be Him."

"We do, we just don't worship him." He hoped he wouldn't offend her, but he could tell from her cocked eyebrow that his explanation didn't make sense. "It's um... we don't think he ever used a rake."

She stopped in her tracks. "I'm sorry, Sanu. I had no idea." A smirk crept up, elevating her whiskers. "Do you trust me?"

"Y-yeah," Sanu stuttered.

"Then let me borrow your scimitar."

"I... you'll give it back, right? It's all I have left of my family. This was my dad's."

A robed novice seedling approached, turned up his snout, and walked by without a word. Sanu pawed his blade over to her.

"Of course, now come a little closer," Cladh said.

Sanu's mouth dried as he inched forward. Cladh grabbed his shirt and pulled him closer. Sanu's heart raced as she lifted his scimitar, then lowered it so the edge rested on the coat of arms stitched into his yellow tunic. She laid the point on one stitch, then tugged the thread loose.

"Now, if anyone asks, I just don't want to seem like I'm supporting Lady Marjitay or asking you to. And you have the benefit of not having to swear to any Frenglese nobles. I'm definitely not doing this to remove Ganan's rake. Besides, since you're learning the language so fast, everyone wants to meet you."

She worked through each stitch until the hated coat of arms fell to the floor. Sanu smiled. Jab would have been ecstatic to get that symbol off his chest, and Sanu was equally happy to be that close to Cladh.

Not that Sanu cared.

"Thank you, Cladh."

"Don't mention it. Now come on, we have to get outside. I have some bad news."

"Bad news?"

She stopped in front of the stairs and let out a tight exhale. "There was an attack last night, Sanu. A whole outpost—killed or missing. One of Nasalid's emissaries is waiting at the gate to negotiate. Because they raided a Gananshed and have all the holy things, it's up to the Sapling to receive him. The Sapling wants a team of translators, not just me." She climbed and her tone softened. "It'll be nice not to have all the pressure on me. It's also nice that Lady Marjitay can't make the decision."

"But I can't speak Frenglese. I guess I could say and understand a few phrases, but—"

She nudged him gently. "Don't get a big head. Yagub will join me. Sir Brouglas insisted you join so you and he can learn the languages a little more."

At the top of the stairs, Sanu sidestepped to allow another robed novice seedling to pass. "Not that I have a reason to, but nobody is worried I'll leave and join Nasalid?"

At the mention of the Liberator, the novice seedling glared at Sanu.

Cladh smiled. "Somebody did bring that up, but Sir Brouglas insisted you wouldn't." Her tone and expression darkened. "You saw how Nasalid burned rodents alive. You know what he'd do to Olihort and why that can't be allowed to happen."

ZelZaytun in flames. The sacred Gnaverwood tree reaching through the clouds, desecrated. Even without being a devout Grovekeeper, the possibility shook him to his core. Maybe Nasalid was a liberator for politics, or military, or whatever, but not the holy city of ZelZaytun. To think he'd once thought of the man as a hero.

The beaver knight and squirrel squire met them outside the Gananhall. Sanu unconsciously went to put a paw over his eyes to let them adjust to the light, but he realized that with all the natural lighting and windows inside the Gananhall, his eyes didn't need to, even with the polish of Sir Brouglas' armor.

The quartet marched through ZelZaytun, too fast for Sanu to drink in the city's beautiful sights. Upon reaching a break in the city walls, a worker porcupine hauling a rickshaw made Sanu stop in his tracks. Inside this wooden rickshaw was an olive bigger than Sir Brouglas' tail. It must have come from the sacred tree.

Yagub, the beaver knight, and Cladh also stopped, bowing as the olive passed them by.

As if something like that could be an object of worship more than the One who planted it in the first place.

"We have to hurry," Yagub said. "Sanu, I imagine that looked strange to you. I can explain later, but we have to go."

"Go...fast," Sir Brouglas called, marching ahead.

Cladh took Sanu by the paw and pulled him along to catch up.

Such a disrespectful thing, to even handle an olive from the sacred Gnaverwood, and yet they acted like the All-Planter's own tooth rolled by them. Sacrilege for a Grovekeeper was holy to a Sprouter. That rickshaw driver would take the olive to the bakery, where it would be remade into food. The idea made Sanu cringe. Jab would scold him for looking down on another faith's practices. Yet knowing what these rodents would do to the sacred olives made it clear this city might not be shareable. How could a Grovekeeper stand idly by while a Sprouter takes something from the sacred grove? And how could a Sprouter practice their faith without doing that very thing?

After what felt like an hour of marching through the sacred city, circling the holy tree's sacred, walled-off grove, they reached ZelZaytun's gate. This road would lead to Rattin. Yet the opening gate didn't invite him to run home. He didn't have one to run back to without burdening Rijat and being the subject of even more pity. Orphaned and without a brother. There wasn't even a word for anyone that pathetic.

Standing on the opposite side of the gate was an entourage of rodents that looked like they could've been distant relations. Two brown squirrels, scimitars in paw, astride beautiful nimble horses. They carried the red-white checkered flag of discussion, an understanding shared by interpreters and readers from both faiths. These squirrels were here to discuss, not surrender.

A pair of jerboas trotted between them, one wearing the plumed helmet of a lieutenant and swinging his tail, which had a bludgeon tied to the end of it. Judging by the number and size of his scars, he looked like he'd seen war all his life. The other jerboa seemed the opposite, dressed as a noble in fineries and silks. He was accompanied by a squire, holding Nasalid's golden wolf banner. Behind the quartet was a donkey and cart, driven by a gerbil. The cart was covered and looked laden.

Sir Zantiz had beaten them there. Sanu almost didn't recognize him outside his armor. Zantiz wore a vest modified for his quills. His devilbeak had been swapped for a cane. It was only the voice and fluency that proved this was Zantiz at all.

"Greetings, O emissary of Nasalid," Sir Zantiz announced.

Buzzards squawked above, circling something just outside the gate. If they were any lower, Sanu wouldn't have been able to see them over the city walls. Sanu and his group arrived as the emissary responded.

"And to whom do I speak? I carry the authority and banner of Nasalid, Liberator of Nations." The princely jerboa's accent suggested he was from somewhere far away, maybe from one of the first places Nasalid liberated. Bludgeon-tail scowled, and Sanu wondered how many of Nasalid's battles he'd led the charge on.

Zantiz nodded to Sir Brouglas and Cladh, and waved to Sanu and Yagub. Smiling, he returned his focus to the emissary. "I did not catch your name in that, friend. I am Sir Zantiz, right paw to Lady Marjitay, defender of Olihort."

"Watch your tongue." Princely and the rodents with him sneered at the use of ZelZaytun's false name. Even his horse seemed rattled. "Your presence here sullies the sacred city. Do not blaspheme further with any other name than ZelZaytun."

"Apologies, emissary. Perhaps I should close this gate since you're so obstinate."

With her gold-crusted acorn amulet swaying with each step, Cladh stormed up beside Zantiz, catching the ire of bludgeon-tail. "Now wait one minute," she told him. "You're not the only one with a paw in this discussion." She turned to the emissary and pointed at her amulet. "I represent the Sapling of—this city. He is ill and cannot speak your language, so he sent me." The emissary and his entourage relaxed a fraction, and Sanu's heart quickened. "This amulet on my neck—I understand this might be meaningless to you, but it means I have permission to speak with his authority."

Zantiz bristled. "And we still do not have *your* name, dear emissary."

Princely scowled at him. "You speak with Difatim, and you would do well to learn the respect this girl shows." Difatim wasn't as good of a name as princely; Sanu decided to cover his ears if anyone said bludgeon-tail's name.

Behind Sanu, Yagub mumbled translations to Sir Brouglas.

Sanu's whiskers twitched. Zantiz had been so nice and curious when it came to discussing and training with Sanu all week, yet he was like a different rodent here.

Difatim continued. "Last night, the Liberator seized your supply station. By his command, no looting took place. All who surrendered are safely in our prison camp, receiving food and water."

Zantiz tapped his cane against the paved stone road. "My lady would want proof of this."

Difatim motioned to the donkey and cart beside bludgeon-tail. "Your Gananshed had objects our experts said were blessed and would be cherished by your seedlings and Sapling. We're here to offer an exchange for these objects and prisoners."

Cladh wedged herself in front of the porcupine. "And what's the request?"

Sir Brouglas stepped beside Sanu. "They... talking... too fast. Is city in... peril?"

Sanu tested his growing Frenglese vocabulary. "Zantiz... not agreeable, but polite. Cladh... agreeable. Not polite." He certainly sounded like an idiot, but he was proud of himself because the beaver knight understood.

The jerboa noble inched his horse forward, as did his squirrel guards behind him. "Lady Marjitay and her ruling nobles must depart ZelZaytun forever. All of your knights and soldiers must evacuate as well. After the Liberator takes the city, he will allow Sprouter pilgrims to visit the city unarmed."

"This is some kind of joke," Zantiz said.

Cladh scowled at the porcupine. "Can I see the objects?"

The jerboa snapped his fingers, and the cart driver pulled back a corner of the covering, revealing glittering gold cups and stylized rakes.

"For us to agree is a problem," Cladh said, indicating Zantiz. "These sacred objects are religious, so what happens to them is a decision belonging to the Sapling."

"And what you ask for in return is a political decision." A confidence rang through Zantiz's voice that Sanu didn't understand. "You killed the prisoners already, didn't you, Difatim?"

Bludgeon-tail snarled at Zantiz, cutting off whatever Difatim prepared to say. "We're not in the business of killing the defenseless." The acid in his voice was unlike anything Sanu had ever heard. "You wouldn't understand that, would you? Standing here in a stolen city."

Cladh approached the emissary, paws open. "Please, we want to move past that. Together. As neighbors."

"Impossible," Difatim sneered. "Not after what was done to the citizens of ZelZaytun."

"Exactly," bludgeon-tail hissed.

Zantiz tapped his cane against the road. "What's impossible is Nasalid setting hindpaw in *Olihort*. The All-Planter's will is that we reside here. Who do you think you are against the power of Ganan the Gardener, Blest Be Him? Who does Nasalid think *he* is? I have a counter-offer for Nasalid. You leave that stolen treasure behind, and Nasalid can crawl back to whatever sand hole he came from."

Sanu's heart raced. The way the emissary's guards clenched their weapons and the lieutenant waved his weaponized tail, this would go down in the worst way possible.

Leaving Sir Brouglas' side, Sanu shouted, "Wait! I'm a Grovekeeper. I was taken in by these knights."

"Wait." Difatim cocked his head, and his whip of a tail spun around. "Are you their prisoner?"

"N-no," Sanu stammered. "They are my friends. I—"

"—have nothing to say to us then. *Traitor.*" The emissary spat, then trotted away.

"I'm not a traitor, you jerk!" Sanu would've preferred being called an orphan. He wasn't even sure who he *could* betray if he wanted to.

Shaking their heads, the armed squirrels and cart driver turned around as well. Bludgeon-tail was the last to leave, spitting in the dirt before turning around on his horse. Even from a distance, the size of his spit seemed impressive. If Mutarra were here, she'd want to examine it to gross everyone out.

"Good riddance," Sir Zantiz muttered.

Cladh wheeled on him and spoke too fast for Sanu to understand, but Brouglas' chuckle suggested she'd said something unrepeatable.

"Sir Zantiz!" The call echoed from the far side of the city gate. Just up the road, the emissary had stopped with his entourage, facing ZelZaytun again.

Once everyone turned to face him, he continued. "See what happens when you insult Nasalid, besmirch the holy city, and turn a Grovekeeper boy against us."

The armed squirrels dismounted, then unhooked a bucket from each of their saddles. They opened the buckets and poured whatever was inside over the cart.

"Last chance. Agree to my terms or bring out Lady Marjitay herself."

"Tell Nasalid to chip a tooth," Sir Zantiz called back.

"No, no! Bring Nasalid here!" Sanu pleaded.

"Bring him here to chip a tooth," Difatim said. "So be it. This is on *your* conscience. Servant girl of the Sapling, know this connection goes back to him," he pointed his long whip of a tail at Zantiz, then Sanu, "and we know you can't be trusted because you've warped a young boy's mind."

"What does he mean?" Sanu asked. Before anyone could answer, the cart was aflame.

Blessed items burned because Cladh and Zantiz couldn't reach a compromise with Difatim, and Sanu's words were the last thing that made Difatim turn around in disgust.

Those blessed items were true garbage, lacking any value to Grovekeepers, but they meant the world to Sprouters. More than that, if they were their keys to the afterlife somehow, this was an insult that couldn't be taken back.

Was that really what Nasalid the Liberator would want? It felt so wrong. Barbaric. Childish. Evil.

No peace would arrive. ZelZaytun would fall under siege.

Whatever Jab would have said or done, Sanu couldn't guess. Fumes and smoke wouldn't carry far enough for him to smell strongly, but he couldn't watch any more. He turned away from the burning carnage and melting metal, facing the city he had doomed.

16

JAB

A prayer warden doesn't rule. If one tries to, bar them from any office. Let them clean the streets or remove animal waste and elect a new prayer warden. A good warden wants a good relationship with rulers, but not to become one. When rulers and wardens are separate and in harmony, peace reigns. When one wishes to become the other, ruination follows.

- Raticenna's Commentaries

Jab breathed deep, reliving the screams. Crunch of bone. Squish of organs. The goose. The now-orphaned goslings—at least they had their brothers.

His teeth chattered and he shivered. Imaginary sounds filled his ears, and the weight of the sleepless night burdened him.

A wet cloth pressed against his head. Kash's voice came muffled through the imaginary cacophony. "His battle nightmares are my fault. Can you help him?"

A vaguely familiar voice answered. "Don't blame yourself." A rustle of twigs in a beard followed. This was Maimon, the red squirrel, personal physician to Nasalid. "Open your eyes, young Jab of Rattin."

With a shaky breath, Jab opened them. He was in Kash's tent, but the other scouts were absent. Kash's headwraps were off, revealing matted brown fur around his ears.

Maimon hunched over Jab, face stern. "You saw rodents die last night in the line of battle?"

Jab squeaked out a quiet, "Yes."

"And you recently had to bury your parents." Maimon's voice was kind, despite his hard expression.

The knot in his stomach swelled. "Yes, sir."

"I heard your brother died too."

Jab considered mentioning that he once lost a pet turtle if there were any other scars Maimon wanted to pick at. "Also true."

"I *told* Difatim and Jorjim not to let you go," Maimon mumbled, stroking his beard, fingers navigating around the twigs intricately woven into it. "It's difficult when you cannot get closure on a loved one. You could not do any ritual for him. Then you saw battle-death. Kash tells me you are a young scholar. Is this so?"

"I ... like to read and learn about the Divine Poetics."

The physician smiled. "A beautiful tome."

That snapped Jab into focus, yet Kash seemed unfazed. "I'm sorry, I thought you were a Mulcher," Jab said.

The red squirrel wiggled an ear. "You thought right. I do not need to pray when you do or share your beliefs to respect them and find the Divine Poetics beautiful. It's a fitting title; the poetry is immaculate. We're all praying to the same All-Planter, even if you call Ilha Melek ZelZaytun or a Sprouter says Olihort. We just have different paths to Her."

"Her?" Jab was more curious than offended.

"Or Him. Or It. If the All-Planter is perfect and beyond our full understanding, the All-Planter must be beyond our ability to articulate. Any words we use will always fall short. I hope no rodent is pompous enough to think he can encapsulate the Almighty with the same language we use to discuss chickens and boogers."

Jab chuckled, but stopped when he realized he'd never considered that before. Though unusual, nothing seemed wrong in Maimon's statement. "But I thought Mulchers didn't really believe in the All-Planter." Feeling his cheeks flush, he added, "because you don't believe in the Walled Garden, right?"

Maimon took a long gaze at Jab, examining him with a measured expression. "Of course I believe in the All-Planter. But I can't know what happens after we die. You seem to have an unfortunate streak of loved ones dying around you. Is that why you're asking? Worried about your parents, your brother, or the soldiers?"

Jab stared at his hindpaws. So much death. The pain dug at him and kept his mouth shut.

"I think you're good to stand, lad. Come on." Maimon offered his paw. After Jab accepted it, he continued. "I know the Divine Poetics and Ganan reference the Walled Garden. The afterlife is a belief Mulchers do not share with Sprouters and Grovekeepers." A slow smile spread across his snout. "Our Kingsbooks do not mention the afterlife, which gives us space to find our own ideas."

"If there's no afterlife, what do you have to live for?"

Maimon let out a kind chuckle. "That's where you're wrong, wise one. If there is no afterlife, there is everything to live for. What's different is there's nothing to *die* for." Maimon curled his tail around a water flask. "Drink. Your time to fast will be soon, so enjoy a daytime beverage while you can."

After Jab accepted it and drank, he wiped some excess water from his lips. "Why do you follow Nasalid if you're a Mulcher?"

"He treats me well. I keep him healthy and give him advice when he asks for it. Why should our faith matter in such an arrangement?"

"I ... guess it doesn't."

"Correct, wise one. I enjoyed a discussion with a Grovekeeper scholar. I hope we have many more." Maimon blocked the exit to the tent. The concern in his eyes lightened Jab's spirit. "Are you feeling better?"

"A little." The stomach knot hadn't shrunk, but didn't feel so tight either.

"Don't preoccupy yourself so much with the state of souls. All we can do is our best and to teach others to do the same. Are you ready to go outside?"

The goose feathers, and the flames which consumed Sanu flashed in Jab's mind, but he offered a weak "yes" and "thank you."

They stepped outside, where Kash was waiting, headwraps back on. Jab blinked hard at the sight. He hadn't realized Kash had slipped out.

"I almost came in to get the two of you." Kash's eyes were wide over a wider grin. "Come to the Liberator's tent. Difatim has returned."

Between the rows of tents, four rodents approached, three on horseback and one astride a donkey.

As they neared, soldiers and camp followers emerged from their tents and stopped their morning chores to form a semicircle around Nasalid. Everyone parted to let Maimon through, which allowed Jab and Kash to come to the front, beside the Liberator and his top warden advisor.

Closer now, other soldiers began to murmur. "Where's the cart of treasure they left with?"

"It's gone?"

"We could have melted all that garbage and sent the gold home to our families!"

What struck Jab more than the missing cart was their ragged and tattered clothing.

They'd been attacked. Soldiers around them murmured—the treasure cart, meant to bargain with the Sprouters, had been stolen. Jab couldn't believe that he wished bandits were the culprits instead of the Sprouters. A bandit attack at least would mean negotiations remained a possibility.

Nasalid addressed them. "Jorjim, Difatim, I'm relieved to see you in one piece. I want to hear what news you have, but do you require medical attention?"

"No, Liberator," Difatim said, breathing hard. "We escaped with our lives and steeds. We have mere scratches."

"Then let's discuss what happened," Nasalid replied, voice heavy. "Dismount and let's go to my tent."

Difatim straightened. "No."

A collective gasp rang through the crowd.

"My liege, our troops deserve to know the full tale."

While the crowd's focus was on the noble jerboa who'd refused their general, Jab fixated on Nasalid. The jird clenched his fist and his whiskers twitched. "So be it, but we *will* have a private conversation about this."

"I understand, Liberator." Difatim raised his head to address the crowd. "You all saw us depart under the flag of peace and discussion. I went to negotiate. But you all have heard legends of the Sprouters' cruelty, especially in ZelZaytun. Once they learned what we had, they descended upon us to retake the treasure. They stole it all from us."

More gasps and murmurs reverberated.

Nasalid balked. "Did you tell them we would share the city, that they could remain there, the proposed joint government, open access to pilgrims of all faiths?"

Jab scratched the back of his head. That was such a generous offer. A reasonable one too. Nobody would have to fight over the city anymore.

"I spoke every word true," Difatim said. "I represented you as best as possible."

On Nasalid's other side, Yark the prayer warden scoffed, almost too soft for Jab to catch. Jab wondered if the gerbil advisor to Nasalid had some issue with Difatim.

Without thinking, Jab stepped forward. "They attacked you without warning, or even a counteroffer?" Eyes from all over bored into him, and Jab wished to disappear.

"They were like wolves, *boy*," Difatim said before turning his attention back to Nasalid. "Thankfully, their greed was such that they focused on the treasure instead of our throats." The noble addressed the crowd again. "This is what the Sprouters will do to our precious city! Rip it apart and kill us mercilessly."

The murmurs in the crowd deepened to snarls.

Nasalid sighed, then moved beside Difatim. "Gentlerodents, this is not the course of events I wanted. I had hoped to avoid spilling blood in the holy city. I earned a reputation for ruthlessness in my early campaigns. I wanted to atone for my wrongdoing by restoring ZelZaytun to the Grovekeepers. I thought the All-Planter willed for the city be taken peacefully." He pinched the bridge of his snout. "I'm distraught to see I was wrong about the occupiers. I had hoped to find reasonable rodents. They will rue the day. We'll prepare siege engines and find locations for a forward base. As for the prisoners we took from the battle, leave them undisturbed. They will not suffer because of their leaders' foolishness and sacrilege. We'll reconquer the city before the fast."

Another chorus of mumbles emerged. Some soldiers nodded, understanding, but others scowled at the Liberator as he passed them.

"Come along, Jab," Kash said. "We need to scout the best locations to place the siege engines around ZelZaytun."

Jab coiled his tail knowing soldiers would march over his parents' gravesite.

17

SANU

As a witness, Sanu's presence was required at the summit between the Sapling and Lady Marjitay. Lady Marjitay forced the Sapling, Brouglas, Cladh, Yagub, and Sanu to convene in her throne room, not the Sapling's office.

Yagub explained this put Lady Marjitay in a position of power before the discussion even started. Brouglas pointed out this was preferable to getting their heads removed for botching the negotiation, although she could be summoning them to do just that.

Sanu couldn't understand why people would care about positions of power when they were on the same side, but the politics the Sprouters had with their nobles and clergy remained a mystery.

Back in the royal chamber, Sanu noticed the large portrait of Lady Marjitay brandishing her ornate crossbow. The artist had taken a few creative liberties in hiding her blemishes and crooked teeth.

On their way in, they had to pass the gaudy thing, which occupied much of the wall. Sir Brouglas nudged Yagub. "Even the best artist couldn't make her look noble."

Sanu remembered hearing a trader say mole rats used to live underground while squirrels once lived in trees, and even though it sounded laughably stupid, he wouldn't fault anyone for hiding from the sun with a face like Lady Marjitay's.

The Sapling, an aging porcupine with worn-down quills, shushed Brouglas. "Don't criticize her appearance. You're a knight." His outfit was a pure brown backless shirt underneath a conical hat adorned with acorn shells in the same style as Cladh's amulet. His smile radiated a genuine kindness.

"You could use a bit more diplomacy, Your Excellency," Cladh whispered.

Something in the way she said "excellency" made Sanu smile, maybe from his understanding a big word or from Cladh's small bite of sarcasm.

Armed guards blocking the door parted way upon seeing Sir Brouglas and the Sapling.

Lady Marjitay sat in the twig-decorated throne, drumming her fingers against the arm-rest. Beside her, Sir Zantiz wore full plate armor, devilbeak in paw. He didn't look the image of a hobbled old man anymore, but someone ready to march into battle.

Brouglas murmured about how he should've worn his own armor, which made Yagub sigh.

Understanding them all a little better lifted Sanu's spirits, yet his stomach twisted. The Honking Goose of Olihort was legendary in Rattin for her cruelty and hatred of Grovekeepers. Sanu had said the last word to Difatim, the rep-resentative of Nasalid, the so-called Liberator. With a deep huff, he wondered what he could've said differently, or better yet, what would've hap-pened if he'd remained silent.

Maybe instead, Difatim would be in here right now and on better terms, in the Sapling's Gananhall. No good Grovekeeper would disre-spect another faith inside their holy building. Their whole faith was built on the peace that happens between nations and individuals who respect those who are different. Maybe Difatim had forgotten that, or worse, Sanu's words sent him over the edge.

All roads led back to this being Sanu's fault.

And he had to admit that in front of Lady Marjitay, of all rodents. But he wasn't about to get his head chopped off.

The mole rat's attendant greeted each of them in turn, beginning with the Sapling, then

Cladh and Brouglas, ending with Yagub and Sanu. Sanu wondered if they would add "the orphan" after saying his name.

Sir Zantiz spoke next. "Yes, yes, it is good to see you all after that antagonistic and threatening rhetoric from that horrific noble yesterday."

Horrific?

An unarmed jerboa on a horse wasn't a threat to anybody. The two guards could only defend him, not attack anybody, especially not anyone in a fortified city. Even bludgeon-tail couldn't take on an entire detachment of city guards.

Sir Brouglas stepped forward and pointed a finger at Zantiz but addressed Lady Marjitay. "He bullied the emissary on purpose. Zantiz provoked him, lady."

Sanu couldn't believe his own gift for language. He never would've learned this about himself if it weren't for his time with the Sprouters. Zantiz was using big words, but Sanu followed what he said. He was so proud of himself that a soft chuckle escaped.

All eyes turned on him. Lady Marjitay leaned toward Sanu and pointed. Despite her shrill voice, Sanu understood every word.

"What is so funny, boy? You are the reason the emissary trotted off." Knives scraping ceramics produced more beautiful music than her voice. Her voice might be the last thing Sanu ever heard.

The Sapling stiffened his quills, and the room silenced. "That is not how Acolyte Cladh tells it. I have witnesses to prove Zantiz was the one to upset the emissary."

Sanu gulped and considered which words to use carefully. "I ... wanted to say to the jerboa ... that everyone has had kindness with me. I wanted ... to help. I am sorrowful."

"That was pretty good," Yagub whispered. Switching languages, Yagub addressed the mole rat. "Lady Marjitay, did you understand him? He wished to tell the emissary of our kindness as a show of good faith to assist in the negotiations."

"Yes," Sir Brouglas said. "You should thank this boy and discipline your barking hound. What happened to you, Zantiz?"

"I don't know what story they've imagined, my lady." Zantiz spoke as if this were some meaningless mix up at a sheltercake bakery, like someone used figs instead of dates.

The Sapling spread his quills, and all eyes went to him. "Lady Marjitay, Olihort will face a siege. You are endangering lives. Make peace with Nasalid. The man's chivalry is legendary. This emissary may have been too rash. Let's speak with Nasalid, you and me. We'll each bring translators."

Lady Marjitay scoffed. "Then send a missive back to Gananshire and ask the Arborist for resources and reinforcements to fight Nasalid's rats."

"That would take a month, which is time we don't have. I would sooner send a boatload of Olihort's citizens to an island in Freng where it's safe."

Sanu's fur stood on end. For the Sapling to abandon the holiest city in the world to them must mean he took the threat of Nasalid's siege seriously. Nasalid must possess an equally powerful reputation back on Freng, maybe not as a liberator, but as a powerful warrior and master tactician.

If everyone in the city died, what would happen to Sanu's new friends? They were the good ones. They wanted peace.

"Never," Lady Marjitay said. "We'll empty the other fortifications and attack Nasalid's troops as he prepares his siege engines."

"Is this a joke?" Sir Brouglas asked.

The noble mole rat's whiskers twitched. "Those castles and forts are meant to defend Olihort. It's time the knights there do so, Sir Brouglas. As your liege, I command you to visit the castles and bring the knights here."

After a sorrowful gaze toward the Sapling and Cladh, the beaver knight's shoulders slumped. "I ... will, my lady."

"You can't be serious." The Sapling stiffened, but it didn't command the instant pause among the other rodents like it had earlier. "Lady Marjitay, I won't have you condemn this city to die. At our next Offering Meal, I will tell everyone who attends about what has transpired. I will tell them to leave the city."

The mole rat rose from her chair, scowling. "I rule this city, not you. I am who the All-Planter wants on the throne."

Sanu turned to Yagub and mouthed, "Did I hear that right?"

Over the growing shouting match between mole rat and porcupine, Yagub replied, "If the All-Planter wanted someone else on the throne, her father would've had different children. 'Divine right.'"

"Perhaps He placed you on the throne as a test of faith for the rest of us." Acid dripped through the Sapling's voice. The attendants again averted their eyes from the lady. "There are other, more qualified nobles in Freng who could replace you. Prince Ridgerd comes to mind."

Something in that unfamiliar name rattled everyone in the room except Lady Marjitay and Sanu.

Lady Marjitay exhaled and sat back down. "You know, Your Excellency, you seem a bit tired. Perhaps a seedling could attend to the next Offering Meal in your place. You might need some rest and protection." She snapped her fingers and two of her guards approached the throne. "You two, escort the Sapling back to the Gananhall and ensure he remains undisturbed while he ponders his next decisions and reconsiders the insults he's thrown at me today."

As the guards neared the porcupine, Cladh jumped in front of them. "Don't you dare."

"And get that hamster girl to an unoccupied chamber," Lady Marjitay said, wiggling her whiskers. "We can't let anyone else be subjected to her blabbering. We'll keep you safe, dearie." Her tone melted to mockery.

Another guard emerged and grabbed her.

"No!" Sanu shouted.

Yagub caught him. "They'll imprison them, but they can kill us. Let's not give them any reason."

This was too much. A tear welled in Sanu's eye. He looked at the beaver knight, hoping Sir Brouglas would do the knightly thing and save them, but he held his face in his paws. Sanu had already lost his parents and Jab, and now Brouglas was being sent away.

"Sir Brouglas, begin with Kraksnout Castle and order them here," Lady Marjitay said.

Yagub gasped. "The round trip will take weeks!"

Marjitay waved his comment off. "Leave first thing in the morning. If you discover Nasalid's engineers, attack them. If not, fortify the city." Her tone shifted to mockery. "I think that is the only way the Sapling and hamster girl will recover from their illness. You'll be remembered as the savior of Olihort."

"Understood, my lady," Brouglas intoned.

The beaver knight faced Sanu and Yagub, exposing the line of tears streaking his fur.

18

JAB

- Divine Poetics

On today's scouting run, Jab was trusted with a heavier pack—a paltry reward for flawless crossbow practice. Kash burdened him with measuring instruments. Their mission was to find a suitable location to place the catapults, or at least a group of them, around ZelZaytun, since they were nearing completion. As the countryside became more familiar under his hindpaws, a piece of him grew more appreciative of why rodents would fight over such a beautiful land.

Even without the sacred Gnaverwood, ZelZaytun had to be the most beautiful city in the world.

Construction sped along with the help of Nasalid's engineers, and the supply of fish filling everyone's bellies. Not much activity happened around ZelZaytun in the two days since Difatim returned after the robbery.

Approaching the city in the midday sun became easier than Jab's last few trips; he'd learned how to hold his head and neck so there was no chance of accidentally gazing upon the holy tree. Kash had even showed him a few self-defense moves. They were only for making quick escapes, but it was still exciting to have the skillset. While he still did this and the crossbow training for Sanu, it was becoming a fun challenge. Sometimes he hummed a tune to accompany the *racka-click* of the cranking crossbow gears.

Jab and Sanu had talked many times of how they wished for a secret older brother to appear one day—mostly to mediate their fights, but also for a mentor to help them navigate life, or at least their parents. Kash would have been a phenomenal brother; he definitely looked the part.

Still, Kash proved himself a great guide and friend. And any kid from Rattin would've killed for a chance to get inside Nasalid the Liberator's tent.

They came to a clear patch with a view of the city's south wall. There would be a low chance of a projectile hitting the Gnaverwood tree at this distance.

Kash showed Jab how to stick his thumb out for a quick measurement. "Move your thumb so you cover the tip of the intended target. For us, it's that wall."

Jab complied, eyeing the path. A section of the wall disappeared behind tan fur. "But why not the tower?"

"That tower was built by King Suleimouse. The Liberator does not want any landmarks or historical places destroyed, along with any Ganansheds, the Gananhall, or any Mulcher gathering houses, if they still remain. If we can dismantle enough of the city walls, we'll enter."

"So why this distance?"

"That's the..." Kash snapped his attention to the left and put a finger over his lips to shush Jab. They turned, facing a rustling bush. A gosling stepped out, squawked, then waddled away.

"Sorry," Kash said. "I guess I'm jumpy."

"It's alright." Gazing upward, Jab factored the sun's position. "Can we pray before we measure?"

"Of course. It's about that time."

They stooped down and traced a tree in the dirt, then removed their headwraps, placing them over the tree like a bough of leaves.

Shielding their eyes from the sacred city, they intoned the invocation, asking the All-Planter for forgiveness.

More rustling came from behind. Must have been another goose. Silly creature. As they started the prayer's second portion, pawsteps thudded behind them.

Then the scrape of metal-on-metal followed.

Kash stopped the prayer and shoved Jab hard, making him roll away.

Clang!

Kash's dagger was an inch away from his face, parrying a sword strike.

A Sprouter scout, a porcupine, had found them. He wielded a one-pawed sword, perfect for a fast hit. He wore light leather armor modified for his quills, unlike the heavy metal Jab would've expected. That meant this guy was fast. Jab wished he could see his parents and Sanu again, but not in the afterlife.

Jab prepared his dagger and rushed forward. Kash's eyes widened at the sight of Jab, dagger aloft. The porcupine followed his gaze and shook his head at Jab.

Whoosh!

A muscled arm came at Jab from the side, lifting him off the ground. He'd been caught too. Unable to see his attacker fully, the bushy tail suggested this was another squirrel.

The porcupine who'd pinned Kash shot eyes at Jab's captor, and Kash dropped his dagger. Without moving his sword, the porcupine spoke in a Frenglese accent. "Spies? Scouts? Saboteurs? You're from Nasalid's army, yes?" His fluency in their language felt unnatural. Wrong, somehow. The accent wasn't the only oddity; porcupines weren't from around here.

Stone faced, Kash exhaled slowly. "We are Sprouters. We're locals from the village down the way. Our father was killed in the attack on the supply depot, and we've been running ever since, desperate to get somewhere safe."

The squirrel holding Jab pulled out a dagger and held it to Jab's throat.

Snarling, the porcupine inched closer to Kash. "Think we're stupid, do you? I see your headwraps. We snuck up on you while you were praying. Give us useful information about Nasalid or your little brother is going to lose his body parts, one at a time."

Clenching his fists, Jab fought the urge to cry or shout. He had to trust Kash.

"We heard you coming and thought you were the enemy," Kash said. "Our headwraps have been our cover. Nasalid's scouts and soldiers are everywhere. We wear their garb so they don't harm us. I'm not even sure we've been wearing them correctly."

"Smart, if it's true," the porcupine said. "How did you escape Nasalid?" His tone had shifted, but the placement of his sword remained, hovering over Kash's face.

"My brother has horrible dreams. I took him for a walk to soothe his nerves. When Nasalid descended, we were a safe distance away, but close enough to see our father fall. Look at my brother, even the sight of your sword is making him relive that horrible night."

And there it was. He had permission to cry. Jab stopped fighting and allowed the tears to flow.

Tears for his parents. Tears for Nasalid's soldiers who died in the supply depot attack. Tears for Sanu. Tears for whatever these Sprouter soldiers were about to do to them.

Scowling, the porcupine inclined his head toward Jab's captor, and the burly squirrel let Jab fall.

"What can you tell us about Nasalid then?" the porcupine's quills shook like spears.

Kash stuttered, and the porcupine leaned closer.

With fresh dirt in his eyes, Jab brushed away the tears. "He's massing his forces on the other side of the city. It's why we came here. He's planning to attack the Gnaverwood to force us to leave. He knows how important it is to us."

Sheathing his sword, the porcupine leaned toward Jab. "That doesn't make sense. Grovekeepers think the tree is holy."

All Jab's fur stood at attention. "Which is why Nasalid knows nobody would ever expect it or defend it. We had to hide."

The porcupine soldier backed off, relaxing.

Jab had lied.

The All-Planter and every messenger of the All-Planter who ever trod the earth had insisted honesty was the surest way to the Walled Garden. The deceiver's path led to the Droughtlands.

"Mm. And where is your mother, boys?" the porcupine asked.

"Fever took her," Kash said. "It's why our father traveled here in the first place. He'd hoped his work for the cause to defend Olihort would earn Ganan's favor, letting her into the Walled Garden."

With a soft chuckle, the porcupine's tension left. "Your father would've gotten along with mine. Lads, we aren't able to escort you to Olihort at the moment, but you ought to go. It'll be safe from Nasalid, I swear to you. Ask at the gates to be taken to my home. I will have a bed for you to share and some food while you figure out your next move. I am Sir Zantiz. When I slay Nasalid personally, I'll have more fortune than I'll know what to do with. We must be off. Stay safe."

As the porcupine who almost killed them retreated into the bush, Jab hurried to Kash's side. The older squirrel wrapped him in a hug. "I'm proud of you. You did well." He dropped his voice to a whisper. "I told the Liberator once that scouts needed acting lessons for situations like these."

Actors weren't liars. Jab told himself he was just an actor, and surely they wouldn't be sent to the Droughtlands, right? And this would potentially save lives. A dark part of him wondered what other rules he'd break in the name of doing the right thing.

Clop-clop-clop

Jab's ears stiffened.

Cloppa-cloppa-cloppa

He'd heard that before—lots of hooves.

"There!" Kash shouted, pointing.

Below them, Zantiz and the squirrel with him had mounted a pair of horses and joined a squad of other mounted soldiers.

The band rode past Jab and Kash, forming a thin wall between them and the engineer corps and construction crew. All of whom would have stopped their work for prayer, maybe even by going into the camp's makeshift prayer house.

Jab's mouth dried. "They're going to attack the camp."

"Impossible," Kash stammered. "That's too small of a force to hit the army."

Jab darted forward but Kash caught his wrist.

The Frenglese Sprouters would descend within moments. "What are you doing?" Jab demanded.

"Saving your life. Maybe theirs too." Kash pulled out his light crossbow and a blue handkerchief from his pouch. He tied the cloth to a crossbow bolt and loaded it.

Dots rose up from the construction yard in the distance—crew rising from prayer.

Racka-click

Fhwit!

Kash cranked his bolt and fired toward Nasalid's main camp. "That's the best way I can sound an alarm."

But it was too late. Screams of slaughter flew from the construction yard, rising with smoke and flames as siege engines were lit ablaze. This raid was never about hitting Nasalid's troops, but instead sabotaging the siege engines and neutralizing support crew.

A war horn blew from camp, and dots rose from the tents, charging toward Zantiz and his raiders.

But using Nasalid's own tactic of hit-and-run, the riders were already stampeding away from the burning construction yard. Jab shuddered.

"Don't blame yourself. The blue-bolted arrow was the fastest way to communicate with the actual soldiers. Attacking during prayer. What a heartless maneuver. This will set us back months."

"Months?" Jab asked, blinking his frustration away. "They built those in a week."

Kash cocked an eyebrow. "I'm surprised someone as pious as you isn't considering our upcoming fast. Nasalid can't have workers going at the same speed in this heat on lower rations. Fighting and working on an empty stomach leads to dying on an empty stomach."

The yearly fast was the ultimate challenge of faith and strength, and now participation meant prolonging a siege and suffering. He'd been imagining celebrating the fast in the holy city to honor his fallen family members. Another dream shattered, all because of the wicked Sprouters from Freng.

19

SANU

All rodents must balance their warrior spirit. In excess, the rodent is a bully. When the spirit is absent, a pushover. True warriors master balance.

- Warrior Maxims

After over a week of journeying to Castle Kraksnout, Sir Brouglas and Yagub allowed Sanu to ride the beaver knight's horse, Vermitch. The aging steed had recovered from the horrors of Nasalid's fire trap, making the horse and Brouglas the only survivors on the Sprouter side. Sanu's heart twisted, wondering if he should count himself among the survivors.

The first Grovekeeper he'd come into contact with since the beaver knight rescued him had immediately shunned him, so upset at Sanu he was willing to provoke a war.

With ZelZaytun too far behind to see anymore, Sanu strained to look ahead on the rocky road. A mile ahead, grass gave way to terrain the same brown as Sanu's fur. "Are we close to Kraksnout Castle?"

Brouglas raised an eyebrow. "Your Frenglese is improving. You're better than I am in Qawari."

"Thank you," Sanu replied. "Practicing has been a good way to pass the time while we've been marching. And I've had some good teachers."

"Not to mention you've been listening closely to everything Cladh says," Yagub chided.

Sanu wanted to protest, but Vermitch clopped hard on a loose rock, forcing Sanu's mouth closed. Cladh was a really good teacher, that's all.

Sir Brouglas laughed. "The boy is just interested in learning from a girl so wise, isn't that right?"

Cheeks flushed, Sanu coughed hard and stared at Vermitch's mane. "Y-yes, she's really wise." The shifting landscape started sloping, and Sanu spied a rising dot in the distance and his smile faded. "Um, what will you say to the soldiers?"

"The truth," Brouglas said. "For there is no other way to the Walled Garden. I will tell them what I have seen, and what kind of rodent I think Nasalid is. I will also tell them what manner of danger the Sapling is in. Like me, these soldiers are more aligned with the Sapling than Lady Marjitay. They care more about *where* she is than *who* she is. But she has the upper paw here. She'll doom us all."

Yagub patted Vermitch's side. "Do you think Nasalid will kill everyone? You escaped the battle of Rattin by luck. Nobody escaped his attack on the lake station, since we don't know if he took any prisoners. He might slaughter everyone in Olihort."

"It's only fair," Sanu said. "The Sprouters did when they conquered Olihort." A lump festered in his stomach, as he remembered his parents and stories of his grandparents. "Every man, woman, and child who wasn't a Sprouter."

A long silence passed. He'd said "Olihort" instead of ZelZaytun. Jab would be disgusted with him. Sanu dropped his chin, unwilling to look at either of his mentors. They'd been so kind, and Sanu kept reminding them of something bad in history they had no part of. Sanu wondered if he was just a burden to them now.

"That's why everyone is afraid," Yagub said. "Whether they admit it or not, every Sprouter knows the holy city was taken in the worst way. There was hope that Nasalid wouldn't re-enact the tragedy, but after Difatim burned the sacred objects and Nasalid burned Olihort's garrison, who knows? Those burnings must've been a show of what he'll do to the city."

"Advisors and emissaries are not the people they represent," Brouglas said. "I know that from representing Marjitay enough times; I've had to make everything sound nicer. Who knows what kind of agenda his advisor had."

With twitching whiskers, Sanu asked what had been nagging him since their meeting with the mole rat. "But if you're so sure she'll lose, why not leave?"

"I shudder to think what will happen if Lady Marjitay loses," the beaver replied. He scowled at the road. "All the princes and kings and warlords of Freng will empty their coffers to retake the city so they can make their claim on history. The Arborist once said that any rodent who aids in the capture or defense of Olihort gets guaranteed passage to the Walled Garden. If Nasalid takes the city, someone will rise up with an army."

He cast sad eyes at Sanu. "I fear for your rodents, Sanu. Grovekeeper towns like Rattin will be the battleground. We have to prevent Nasalid from winning because it'll bring rise to a greater conflict."

"Who do you think would lead the charge?" Yagub asked.

"Either Prince Ridgerd or King Rattarossa. Both have something to prove, and if the tales passed around taverns are true, some aggression issues to work out."

The names were meaningless to Sanu, but the gravity of their words shook Yagub. Maybe Vermitch too, seeing how he tossed his mane, but Sanu knew that was ridiculous.

"I heard tales of Ridgerd," Yagub said. "That he leads his troops from the front. Goes where the fighting is toughest."

"Isn't that dangerous?" Sanu asked. This Ridgerd was a stark contrast from Nasalid the tactician, legendary for his battlefield communication, sending a constant stream of messengers to the front lines, managing the army from afar. The Liberator had earned his battle scars from fighting under his uncle, Warlord Sharah, but a traditional general would lead from the back, in safety. This Prince Ridgerd sounded more like the noble warrior leader Sanu had dreamed of being one day.

"Of course it's dangerous," Brouglas said, snapping Sanu from his trance. "That's why Ridgerd is so respected. And the man is bigger than a troll, which helps."

"How big?" Sanu asked. The dot in the distance grew enough to become a visible outline of a castle, rising from a craggy hill. "Prince Ridgerd, I mean. Not the castle."

Brouglas shuddered. "If the stories are true, he's one of the tallest rodents in all the islands of Freng. He's also a prince, so he can afford the best weapons, armor, and training. I doubt a crossbow bolt to the heart could take him down."

"The joke is that his army is only there to carry his things," Yagub said. Maybe Sanu didn't know the word for "joke," because neither of the older rodents laughed at the comment.

As the silence fell, Sanu marveled at the castle.

Kraksnout Castle looked like an impregnable fortress, defending a route to ZelZaytun, allowing easier access for trade and supplies for the Frenglese. The castle's first level was carved out of the hill itself, turning what was once a formation similar to the Rattin's horns into a sheer cliff. When hearing about this place, Sanu had imagined himself leading a charge with Nasalid's troops, scaling the walls, but seeing it in person, there was no way siege ladders could hope to reach the top.

"Sir Brouglas, why does the castle's second level seem so much smaller?"

"Smaller is relative," the beaver replied. Some levity returned to his voice. "You could fit Rattin and my hometown on that second level, which is the actual castle. What you're seeing coming up from the ground is just the outer wall."

The straight lines of the laid stone were the only way to distinguish this wall from a sheer cliff face.

"The outer wall around the hill prevents saboteurs from getting under the castle itself," Yagub added.

"Saboteur" was a word in Frenglese Sanu knew before he started learning the language, from stories about the Freng invasion, and he realized all his eavesdropping on the traders who peddled in Rattin may have taught him more Frenglese words and phrases before he officially started learning in the last few days.

"That was how General Ironseed won the battle of Firstcastle," Sanu said.

"Your name for him was General Ironseed, huh?" Brouglas asked.

"He's a folk hero here," Yagub said.

They must have had a different name for him in Freng. Not too much of a surprise—Sanu bet the Sprouters hated him for how difficult he made the conquest of ZelZaytun. The first Sprouter armies to land would have conquered the whole island if it weren't for his leadership.

He was a failed savior, but also the reason rodents put their hopes in Nasalid now.

Closer now, Kraksnout Castle's details came into view. A field of grass separated the fortified wall and the second level. If any attackers did summit those walls, they'd have a long way to go in a clear line of arrow fire, and they'd never get any rams or catapults up with them. If they brought catapults to fire over the walls, the thrown boulders would bounce into grass instead of weakening the walls.

Genius and horrifying.

Sanu understood why Nasalid was giving this castle a wide berth.

At least if the battle was fought here, no civilians would be endangered. Regular people lived in ZelZaytun, innocent of the crimes of others, even if they were Sprouters. Jab would've wanted to make sure they were protected.

Sanu gripped Vermitch's reins tight. "Sir Brouglas, when we return to ZelZaytun, I want to continue my training. When the city is attacked, I want to defend the Gananhall."

Both older rodents arched eyebrows. "You're ... not thinking of taking Sprouter oaths, are you?" Brouglas asked.

"No," Sanu replied. "Cladh told me the city's orphans are taken there, and that's where they live until they are old enough to get jobs or someone adopts them. I want to make sure they're safe in the siege. If any of Nasalid's soldiers arrive, I can explain to them it's just orphans and they'll go somewhere else."

Yagub grinned and replied in their shared language. "A noble protector you'll make. We'll put that scimitar to good use in the training grounds."

20

JAB

You ask why my wardens invite rodents who aren't Grovekeepers to the prayer houses? This is one dif-ference between our faiths. You are a Mulcher because your parents, grandparents, and so on were, much for the same reason you are a gerbil and from this island. While my parents happened to be Grovekeepers, I am one by choice. Even if you stopped believing in the All-Planter, you could not lose your Mulcher identity. Any Grovekeeper who renounces the All-Planter has renounced the faith too. We are like the Sprouters in this way.

- Raticenna's debate
with a Mulcher elder

Jab shuddered, elbowing Kash outside Nasalid's tent. "They're shouting in there."

"The Liberator invited us," Kash soothed. "Sounds like they started early."

They entered as a fist *thwacked* on the table, shaking the figures placed on the map. The larger than average tent suddenly felt much smaller, especially with Nasalid's top advisors gathered.

Nasalid sneered at Difatim. "Speak such words again about Maimon and you will need to find a new Liberator to advise. My brother has asked for a position, and I'm not opposed to giving him yours. Do not take me for my uncle."

Kash and Jab stood against the tent wall, forced to witness Nasalid and Maimon arguing with Difatim and Jorjim. The only one missing was Yark, the head chaplain and engineer.

Standing beside Nasalid, Maimon hung his head. "I do not wish to cause discord. I apologize for what I did that led you to believe such things about Mulchers, Difatim."

"But you *could*," Difatim said. It hadn't taken him long to find a nice, embroidered thobe to wear after returning from being robbed outside ZelZaytun's gates. "You could make a poison. It would only be fair retribution for the slaughter of the first invasion. Not to mention the assault on Kashdood and the savior of Rattin right before the disaster on the siege engines."

Jab wished Yark were here to mediate, but the prayer warden was with the surviving engineers and construction crew. "Um, maybe Yark should be here to weigh in? A prayer warden's opinion would be useful," Jab squeaked.

Kash's elbow came sharp into Jab's side. Difatim and Jorjim glowered at him.

Maimon smiled weakly at Jab and straightened. "Liberator, I could concoct a strong poison, as Difatim suggests. I know the foul rumors about Mulchers, but I can assure you, it's not from any dark magic—only straightforward science."

"Prove it," Difatim hissed.

"Bite your tongue!" Nasalid hissed back.

Waving a paw, Maimon went to a chest in the corner of the tent where he kept his medical supplies. "Don't bother, Nasalid." He rifled through his belongings. "It's good for the boy to hear the rumors said about Mulchers. Then he can compare what he hears to what he sees and make his own judgment."

"I think a *real* Grovekeeper would treat Mulchers with respect," Jab said.

With a wry smile that lifted the woven twigs in his beard, Maimon held up a slip of parchment. After pawing it to Difatim, he cocked a grin. "There. Recipe for a poison. Not evil Mulcher magic. I'll take your silence as an apology."

Nasalid pinched the bridge of his nose. "I do not doubt your abilities, Maimon. I will not poison ZelZaytun's water supply."

Difatim squinted at the parchment. After a long moment, he returned it to Maimon. "I apologize for the insinuation, Maimon. Your science is *so* advanced it seems like magic to a mind as *small* as mine." The noble shook his ornamented head and scowled at Nasalid. "But I won't apologize, Liberator. I will speak plainly. There are no innocent rodents in ZelZaytun. There are only soldiers, the Sapling, and Lady Marjitay's servants."

"And no Sprouters are innocent," Jorjim added, flicking his tail and letting the bludgeon roll against the rug.

Nasalid waved them both off. "I will hear no more of this. Even if what both of you claim is true, we cannot risk poisoning the Gnaverwood. We will not damage the sacred tree."

"Grovekeeper soldiers will die taking the city," Difatim warned. "How much blood do you want on your paws? How will we avenge the construction crew? All their hard work is gone."

"Blood spilled valiantly is better than poisoned sap from the Gnaverwood," Nasalid replied. "I've done enough to anger the All-Planter. The Sprouters will only invade again if we damage the tree, and we'll lose our support among the Grovekeeper nations. Attacking without siege weapons is tantamount to failure. We will have to rebuild during the fast and attack next month." His attention shifted to Jab and Kash. "If Sprouter scouts are actively patrolling the area, we must exercise caution in the construction of the siege engines. That area you found must be considered compromised."

If Jab hadn't asked to pray, they wouldn't have been caught, but even more engineers would have died in Zantiz's raid.

"We'll find another spot, Liberator," Kash said.

"No." Nasalid's refusal came out neutral, although clipped. "There's a thicket of trees nearby, yes?"

Jab wanted to mention the goose habitat and stick his tongue out at Jorjim, but that was immature so instead he plotted squeezing lemon juice into Jorjim's water.

"See if it would be possible to put ropes on those trees, so they could be cut quickly. We'll put wheels on the new siege engines and roll them through, covered by the thicket of trees. Then when it's time for the siege next month, we'll cut them down and they'll all fall quickly in the proper direction, thanks to those ropes we'll have tied. See if that would be feasible. You can climb trees, yes?"

"You have the right squirrels for the job, Liberator," Jab said with enthusiasm that would've impressed Sanu. Kash smiled down at him.

"Visit the engineers first to tell them the plan."

With their new orders, Jab and Kash bowed and turned to leave.

"Wait," Nasalid said. "Jab, are there woodcutters in Rattin? Or a skilled carpenter?"

"Yes, a gerbil named Rijat," Jab replied without thinking.

"Good. Kashdood, when you return to the scouts' tent, tell someone to visit Rijat of Rattin. He will have the honor of joining the siege of ZelZaytun."

Since they didn't know about their father's death, Mutarra and Qala had one relative left besides each other, their uncle Rijat. Jab couldn't be the reason he risked himself and entered a battle since he was so willing to offer Jab and Sanu jobs after Mom and Dad died. "Wait, Liberator—he has two nieces he watches over. They need him."

"I see," the jird general replied. "Kashdood, tell the scout Rijat's family will have lodging in the camp. In fact, any rodents of Rattin who can swing a woodcutter's axe should join. Convince the prayer warden they ought to volunteer."

"At once, Liberator," Kash said. With a quick bow, he left, pulling Jab out of the tent with him. Miai supported Nasalid. All the rodents of Rattin did. They'd give everything for ZelZaytun. Jab hoped they wouldn't be giving their lives for it too, all on account of him.

Each row of tents they passed sat empty. Every able-bodied rodent was in the training grounds, gathering and preparing food for when they broke the fast each night, or busy laboring with the engineer corps. On their last day of normal eating, much had to be done while everyone had full energy.

Across the camp, Jab and Kash met with Yark, the prayer warden advisor to Nasalid and chief engineer. His knowledge rivaled Maimon's in different areas of science. Jab had been wanting to ask this gerbil questions about the Divine Poetics and Raticenna's works for days but never received the chance. Not that he could now amid all the rubble and cinders.

Burned springs and gears the size of Jab's body spread out as workers pulled everything together, salvaging what they could from the ruined siege weapons. Many of the horses were assisting the laborers, clearing ash piles. Jab thought he saw Macarona in the mix.

To think these materials would've come together to become a siege engine made Jab wonder what they must look like, or what they had looked like in previous battles. To assemble them just to dismantle them and repeat the process somewhere else felt daunting, but based on the size of some of these wooden planks and beams they'd be impossible to move when assembled.

And now everything was ash and warped metal.

Yark showed Jab a diagram of a completed engine: a wooden triangular frame taller than a tree. Between the standing two triangles, a wooden lever rested, attached to a counterweight that looked like a large basket. The lever was fastened with ropes and other fabrics, and a boulder the size of an army tent sat at the bottom of the lever. The whole contraption resembled a giant arm, readying to throw a stone overhead. The drawing felt unreal.

Yark sighed, rolling the paper up. "I was supposed to oversee construction, checking diagrams and measurements, while also ensuring no worker or soldier overexerted themselves. Now, I'm overseeing the casualty count."

"How many died, warden?" Jab regretted the question as he spoke.

"Very few, but the loss of material was catastrophic. We need new supplies now. But not until after we have a joint funeral tonight and tend to the wounded. But I assume you two are here for another reason."

Kash relayed the Liberator's orders.

"I'm sorry to hear you were ambushed, as well," Yark said. "I lost my tail once in a battle.

Nasalid's uncle made me pretend I was a hamster and spy on the Sprouters." The gerbil chuckled. "It went poorly."

Jab winced before remembering losing a tail was survivable for a gerbil. "But can you rebuild these engines on wheels and roll them to battle?"

"It's slow, but we can after mustering the supplies. The question is if we should sacrifice speed or firepower. Knowing the Liberator, I have an idea."

The word "sacrifice" tugged at Jab. He'd sacrificed his honesty. "Um, Yark? Is it sometimes alright to sacrifice something the All-Planter told us to keep? Like if we were on a mission?"

Yark peered at Jab and Kash's headwraps, then stooped to meet Jab's gaze. "You're a scout. You have to go into enemy lines, and more lives depend on you than is fair. If you're caught by an enemy who will harm Grovekeepers or any innocent rodents, don't feel bad about telling a lie to save a life."

Jab's gaze fell to his suddenly interesting hindpaws. "How did you know I lied?"

"Word travels. Your lie saved your own life, Kashdood's, and possibly many others. The All-Planter judges the intentions behind our actions. I was in your position once—please forgive yourself. You may have to lie again, if you are to become a great scout. Your actions saved lives. Savior of Rattin, indeed."

Jab swallowed hard; it sure didn't feel like he'd saved anything.

He imagined the siege engine on the diagram firing a boulder at ZelZaytun, missing a wall and hitting somebody's house. Maybe if the Sprouters knew of the firepower their engines had, they'd surrender.

A knot formed in Jab's stomach. Lady Marjitay would never surrender. Her army would have to be forced to see reason. Regrettable, but he could see no other way. He had to minimize the impending bloodshed; that would honor his brother and parents.

21

SANU

You've given me two contradictory orders. Save our island and do so with fewer rations. I won't force soldiers to march on an empty stomach. I will not command them, unpaid, to wield a spear. Pardon my bluntness, but send me supplies. The Divine Poetics list the qualities of those admitted to the Walled Garden. Stinginess is not one of them.

- General Ironseed's second letter to the Five Princes of Qawar

Dozens of Castle Kraksnout's knights were local Qawari Sprouters like Yagub, not Frenglese rodents. They could've been Sanu's cousins. Some of them might really have been, as little as he knew about his grandparents. And yet, Sanu was here with Sir Brouglas to give the command to fight Sanu's people. Qawari Grovekeepers.

For the castle's huge size, the interior felt cramped, as if the arched walls were pressing in, ready to cave at any moment. Yagub explained the hallways were cramped—the castle's walls were thick to resist siege weapons on the outside and easier to defend chokepoints with fewer soldiers on the inside. Some walls sported mosaics with scenes depicting Sprouter heroes.

The fort's commanding officer was a grizzled hamster, missing a chunk from an ear and sporting a chipped tooth. He'd probably earned his scars fighting bandits and pirates and was rewarded with leading the garrison here.

Watching the beaver knight explain the situation sent a shiver up Sanu's spine. Brouglas gave Lady Marjitay's order, which roused the soldiers to cheer. Then he explained the Sapling's house arrest, which incensed them.

A squirrel seedling joined the commanding officer, and he seemed more ready to grab a sword and charge than the actual knights present.

Sanu wondered if he had a way to communicate to Nasalid that this castle would be vacant—he could send a small detachment of soldiers to take it and then defend Grovekeepers against any new aggression from Frenglese Sprouters. But Sanu didn't want to endanger Brouglas and Yagub or put Cladh in more trouble. This whole mess made him angry.

Yagub placed a paw on Sanu's shoulder. "Sounds like we'll ride out in the morning. The commanding officer invited us to eat with the other higher officers while they prepare to leave. It's a mistake to abandon this place."

Whiskers drooping, Sanu shook his head. "I'm sorry, Yagub, but I can't eat with you." Images of Jab flashed through his head. It was the month of fasting. But if he drew attention to his Grovekeeper practices, these soldiers might string him up. "My stomach is upset." He had no clue how to keep this up for a month.

Yagub peeked through a window slit meant for an archer to rain death. "Are you sure? We can tell the cook to put in some digestive aids. A squeeze of citrus and spice might solve that."

What would Jab say to Sanu? Pretending like he didn't need to fast and making excuses to cover his faith—the prospect made him nauseous. "Yeah," Sanu said. "I ... might have something before I go to bed. I think the heat got to me on the road here."

Yagub arched an eyebrow and dropped his voice. "It's your day to fast, right?"

"Month," Sanu whispered back. "Would you tell them I'm not feeling well and just need a bed?"

"Of course," Yagub said through a smile. "I'll cover for you and will make sure nobody bothers you. I'll come by after sunset with some bread."

It was hard to find anything to smile about in this stark monument of Sprouters stealing land from Grovekeepers, but having a friend and mentor like Yagub helped. He wished Jab could have met him. They'd always wanted an older brother.

The next morning, the garrison departed, going downhill the whole way. Each step made the holy Gnaverwood in the distance grow taller while the sunrise washed over the road. Despite how large it loomed, they'd still need another two weeks to reach it.

A trader who came through Rattin once told Sanu and Jab that other islands had Gnaverwoods also, some even having multiple, but it sounded like something a bored traveler would say to entertain children, and even the trader admitted they lacked the sacred one's holy mystique. Nothing could rival the magnificence of the olive tree in the distance, even if it wasn't the only giant tree in the world. Yet from here, Sanu's fingertip could conceal it.

If ZelZaytun were taken back and the Sprouter knights retreated to Castle Kraksnout, they would be forced to stare at the tree, more visible than the city around it. The sight would drive them mad with a desire for revenge. Perhaps Kraksnout's placement was at this distance for a reason, just close enough to keep the holy tree in sight.

Could there ever be a peaceful balance again, the harmony he assumed his grandparents knew as kids? It seemed like a fantasy. In the time of the Five Princes, there was no single ruler on this island. Each region ruled differently, but there were supposedly good relationships with the Sprouter and Mulcher minorities. They were fine in their towns and neighborhoods. Maybe the Frenglese islands had a similar arrangement. Or maybe every rodent there was a Sprouter, and the idea of living peacefully with rodents from another religion was inconceivable. Common ground existed somewhere. They'd had it once.

Supposedly.

Maybe all anyone had was an idealized version of their childhood, hearing about their parents' idealized version of theirs, and the past always seemed brighter than it was. Sanu couldn't imagine telling his future children that things were better in his childhood. War, separation, strife, betrayal, mistrust. The list of woes dragged on.

A dark notion emerged: there may be new ways for things to get worse he'd never even imagined. Dread over the unknown made his palms sweat.

The most horrifying thing was how many orphans were under the Sapling's protection in ZelZaytun. They'd be defenseless against Nasalid.

Sanu had no way of letting Nasalid know that there were innocents in the city, but he could protect the orphans. Then, when Nasalid's soldiers arrived, he'd explain everything, and they'd protect the children and go about their business, while Sanu would stop any knight who tried to get in his way.

Filling himself with purpose, a smile bloomed on Sanu's face.

Beside him, Yagub chuckled. "Finally comfortable in the saddle, are you?"

The reins were loose in Sanu's paws, and Vermitch wasn't fighting him as much, just happily plodding forward behind Brouglas and the commanding officer and a wagon driver carrying supplies. Sanu checked over his shoulder. The knights at his back were a garrison, not an army. He wouldn't have known the difference, but he saw it plainly now. The band of knights who died at Rattin numbered around one hundred, and the garrison here was nearly two thousand, but even those combined wouldn't equal a full army. These weren't even all mounted knights, mostly heavily-armored infantry. ZelZaytun was nowhere near Castle Kraksnout's defensibility since it wasn't a military stronghold.

Long days in the saddle lay ahead.

22

JAB

Hear, O rodents! Know I have planted the world and all which dwells in it. When you gaze upon another rodent, animal, plant, or object, you are looking at something from Me. Be respectful of what you eat and mindful of this before you quarrel. Even the rodent you hate most is precious to me.

- Divine Poetics

Axe gripped tight in blistered paw, Jab swung, connecting with his target with a *thwack*. He stepped back from the tree, inspecting the cut on the bark. He wasn't proud of hurting a tree but was proud of himself for making a cut. Kash had explained that this was a guiding cut, so the tree would fall in the intended direction. After a week of measuring between crossbow practice sessions, they'd finished plotting out a path through the cluster of trees which would lead them to an ideal siege engine location for their assault on ZelZaytun.

With the month of dedicated fasting, everything now was preparation for the march onto the holy city, the siege that would push the invaders from Freng back to their home islands, hopefully never to return.

After weeks of rebuilding with half speed and half energy, the construction crews almost had the siege engines ready. A few miles away, Rijat, Miai, and the other Rattin townsrodents were busy cutting and shaping the wood outside the town. This thicket of trees was left preserved, except for Jab and Kash's project.

Kash approached Jab, evaluating the cut. "That was your best one yet. Let's try increasing the pace though."

Jab ignored his throbbing paws. They would make the guide cuts today and come back over the next few days to affix ropes around the tops of the tree trunks to make them fall even quicker. Felling the trees in this fashion felt odd, but Jab relented to the fact that doing everything in batches would save time. Too many trees disappearing in the upcoming days might tip off anybody patrolling ZelZaytun's outer walls. The same outer walls the siege engines would destroy.

He wondered what kinds of rodents were in the city. "Kash, is it really true that only warriors live in ZelZaytun? With the city's size, there has to be other, regular rodents living there."

Kash grunted as he finished his next cut. "Maybe. That wasn't what Difatim said though."

Between swings, Jab grunted, "He didn't have a problem with—*ungh*—asking Maimon to poison the city's—*hrrk*—water."

"You're putting too much emphasis on your hands and wrists. Strength comes from your hips on these swings. I suppose poisoning a city would be dishonorable."

"And he's always trying to push Nasalid to more dangerous—*urrf*—and risky things with the soldiers. And violate the war precepts from the Poetics."

Moving to the next tree, Kash warned, "Remember not to cut too deep, otherwise it's not a *guide* cut but a *cut* cut. I have some unfortunate news for you, my friend."

Jab approached their next marked tree and swung. "What, that I'm cutting faster than you?"

"I don't lie to friends. No, that no military leader has ever followed every single war precept. Nasalid is only trying now because he is worried about how much he *hasn't* in his earlier career. He killed other Grovekeepers in his rise to power. But after a health scare, he wanted to do everything by the Divine Poetics. To everyone's amazement, he's done that so far against the Sprouters. But some innocents will die in war, that's just how things are."

Jab stared at his hindpaws. No innocent people would die if he could help it. "Kash, what's the scouts' job during the siege?"

"We'll relay messages between the Liberator and the field commanders. Why?"

Jab gulped. Sanu had always desired noble warrior status, someone who would protect the innocent, which could be done without enjoying or seeking violence. "Do you think we could sneak into ZelZaytun? Then we could know for sure if there are any innocent people in there."

"The Liberator seems convinced otherwise," Kash said between swings.

"Based on what Difatim and Jorjim said. But won't he need someone to sneak into the city and map out battle plans?"

Leaning his axe against a tree, Kash shook his head. "There are many maps of the holy city floating around. There's no need."

Jab stopped swinging too. "But the Sprouters built new stuff in the last decades, haven't they? What about those new outer walls?"

"You have a sharp mind for tactics, my friend. You'll grow into a fine commander one day."

The part of Jab that wished to become a prayer warden recoiled against the compliment, but the part of him that wanted to make Sanu proud soared. That would've been the ultimate compliment.

"Can we ask Nasalid for permission then? We can use our same Sprouters-in-disguise cover."

"Yes, and I suppose I should start calling you 'brother.' Let's go."

At sundown the next day, they exercised their privilege to break the day's fast with Nasalid. In the tent with them were Difatim, Yark, Jorjim, and Maimon. Even though Mulchers didn't observe the fast, Maimon told Jab he didn't want to eat while everyone around him was abstaining. Maimon said he admired their dedication to the All-Planter and therefore voluntarily joined. Kash allowed Jab to give the proposal.

"And that, Liberator, is why Kashdood and I should be allowed to scout the holy city. Even one innocent life inside should impact your strategy."

Difatim and Jorjim scowled, which Yark noticed.

"Excuse me," the prayer warden and engineer said. "The boy is completely correct. You'd do well to remember you serve the All-Planter." The gerbil leaned forward over the long table to peer at the leader. "For what it's worth, I agree with them. The Sprouters may even have some Grovekeeper prisoners in there we don't know about."

Maimon raised a finger. "Another reason to follow young Jab's suggestion is sparing the innocents would mean less support for a retaliatory invasion from Freng. You would even set yourself apart from other conquerors in the eyes of Mulchers." The twigs woven into his beard clicked against each other.

Nasalid nodded. "And who in Freng would raise an army to retake ZelZaytun if we succeed?"

Difatim's brows knitted, Jorjim's fist clenched, and Maimon bowed his head—all three responded with the same name. "Prince Ridgerd."

The name was meaningless to Jab, but Kash and Yark tensed at the mention.

Nasalid arched an eyebrow. "The war-prince? The giant who leads his troops from the front?" A smile spread across his snout. "I hope the fighting will stop after our successes, but I wouldn't mind testing my mettle against him. But you're also all assuming the Frenglese warlords and princes will stop fighting one another."

"If they have common cause, my liege, they will," Yark said. "They have before. Otherwise we wouldn't be here, and the era of the Five Princes would continue."

A shiver ran up Jab's spine. Even though Nasalid's army was impressive, Jab had no way of imagining how many soldiers could be mustered in one giant push from Freng. He didn't even know how many islands were in that particular chain or their size. Freng was always some far-off place in his mind.

Jab tested fate. "So, may we go?"

Nasalid's expression snapped back to regal and reserved. "You may. I've grown fond of your combined scouting abilities. You've already proven yourselves valuable assets. Kashdood, know that if the All-Planter calls you home while in my service, your family will be rewarded greatly for your exceptional work."

Kash put down his fork and placed a fist over his heart. "You honor me, Liberator."

"And Jab, savior of Rattin," Nasalid continued. "Name the kindest family in Rattin, and I will likewise reward them should your service claim your life."

"Rijat the carpenter and his two nieces," Jab replied. It wasn't even a debate. He wondered how Qala would remember him if he did die under Nasalid's command. Would she consider him a hypocrite or hero?

Nasalid cracked a smile. "I'm already in his debt for how much woodworking he has done for the siege engine and extra supply of arrows. I appreciate your restraint in keeping your survival a secret from Rattin's townsrodents."

"Another good reason to send us to ZelZaytun." Jab wanted to see Qala, show himself off to her. Or at least give Mutarra her doll back. And certainly, thank Rijat for his kindness. If Sanu were here, he'd tease Jab, saying it was mostly for Qala.

"I need no further convincing," Nasalid said. "Cover your tracks and have your disguises ready. See what the Sprouters have done to alter the city's layout and identify the location of any innocents." He glared at Difatim and Jorjim. "And that includes the seedlings and other vowed religious. They will not know our blades. Soldiers only."

"Understood, Liberator," Jab said. Kash slapped him on the back like a big brother.

He'd be entering the holy city, not a pilgrim like he'd always hoped, but a warrior.

23

SANU

- Warrior Maxims

Two weeks from Kraksnout and one day away from ZelZaytun, Sir Brouglas and the commanding officer called for a halt. Yagub had borrowed Vermitch to scout ahead for danger, and he'd returned with a grim expression.

"Campfires and tents," Yagub said to the beaver knight. "Just shy of our left flank, splitting the distance between us and Olihort."

"Sleeping during the day?" Brouglas asked.

"Preparing a siege, no doubt," the commanding officer said. The hamster's rough accent matched his grizzled exterior. "I know why they're sleeping though."

The graying hamster turned to face the garrison and sweat beaded on Sanu's paws as his stomach rumbled.

"These Grovekeepers," the commanding officer said, "they're fasting during the day this month. If they're preparing siege engines, doing it under the cover of night is wise. They were not expecting us to leave Kraksnout. What say we detour and show Nasalid he ought to go back to wherever he came from and leave Olihort to us?"

The seedling raised a fist in the air. "The All-Planter wills it!"

Over one thousand armored fists shot into the air, catching the afternoon sun and shining in Sanu's eyes.

The commanding officer waved. "If they're sleeping, let this be the quietest charge of our lives. We'll bring back their bodies and weapons as gifts for Lady Marjitay while we free the Sapling."

Sanu's heart chilled like the desert night. The garrison changed direction in one step and advanced from where Yagub had come. Sanu was about to witness a slaughter. Sir Brouglas and a huge band of troops who'd been itching for battle were about to do to Nasalid's troops what had been done to the knights of ZelZaytun. Those knights may have been relatives or friends of the Kraksnout garrison. The revenge would be merciless, a slaughter of his countryrodents while *he* was on the other side.

As the troops passed around the frozen Sanu, Yagub navigated Vermitch through them, then leaned forward in the saddle to offer Sanu a paw.

Shaking himself from the daze, Sanu accepted and climbed into the saddle beside his friend who had just secured the death of hundreds of Grovekeepers.

"A victory here might bring us closer to a peaceable solution," Yagub said. "Try not to think of them as Grovekeepers, but a hostile force of people who would starve a city into submission. Sieges are not pretty. Sir Brouglas never told me much about the battle of Phranktonbourg, but it was brutal. That's not something we want happening to Olihort."

Sanu clenched his fists. Yagub would never betray him. Yagub was his brother now. If Sanu wanted to defend the orphanage, he needed to know how Nasalid's troops fought for real. "Let's go. A quick victory will be worth the sacrifice." He wished he could believe his own words.

He blinked a tear away, but he was too slow, and a single drop splashed onto Vermitch's saddle. Yagub steered the horse to face the marching troops while Sanu prayed he didn't notice the new wet spot.

Sanu's stomach convulsed, and it wasn't from Vermitch's galloping. He'd dreamt of warrior status his whole life, but he didn't want to see anybody die. He'd never imagined enemy soldiers as real rodents with families. Steeling himself, Sanu forced his eyes to remain open as they approached the looming battleground. Wispy smoke from campfires rose over the edge of surrounding foothills, and the tips of tents peeked over soon after. Yagub pulled ahead of the marching soldiers, allowing Sanu a view of them from the side.

Porcupines, squirrels, beavers, jerboas, and hamsters, all wearing Ganan's rake on the surcoats covering their armor alongside coats of arms from various noble families—all meaningless to Sanu. They charged forward, eager to kill a sleeping foe. Yagub tugged on the reins, steering Vermitch toward the top of a foothill to observe what would unfold below. A wide ring of tents stood, with smoldering and still-burning fires in between them.

Sanu's eyes widened. There should have been pawprints all over.

As the garrison stormed inside the ring, not one of Nasalid's soldiers emerged from their tents.

When half the soldiers came inside, the commanding officer ordered them to investigate the tents, swords at the ready. Yagub watched them enter, but Sanu's eyes drifted. No horses. Or large chunky and reedy signs of horses splotched the ground nearby. There weren't any stowed weapons or cooking pans near the fires.

Sanu blinked hard. "Is the camp abandoned? Was it ever even occupied?"

"If there's a fire, there's a camp. Unless this is a trap and I'm a really bad scout."

Soldiers emerged from the tents, shrugging. Sanu didn't know enough of their accents to understand everything they said, but the word "empty" stuck out. This camp was a decoy.

"Why would Nasalid waste tents and firewood?" Sanu asked. Jab would have some smart philosophical answer if he were here.

From the center of the false camp, the commanding officer pointed a spear toward Yagub. "Deceiver!"

The seedling shouted something at Yagub, too fast for Sanu to translate in his head. He hadn't heard the word before, but from the context, his guess was "traitor."

Sir Brouglas jogged over, placing a paw on the officer's raised spear. Whatever the beaver knight said seemed to calm the officer, but the seedling's teeth chattered with rage.

"Take the reins, Sanu," Yagub said, slipping off the saddle.

Yagub opened his paws, exposing his palms. "I am sorry, friends. From afar, this camp looked inhabited. The Liberator wanted us to get sidetracked, I think. Or they saw us coming and evacuated."

Heart racing, Sanu wondered if they'd strode into a trap. Yagub wasn't a traitor, that was for sure.

Soldiers removed their helmets to reveal sweat-soaked heads, white lips, and sunken eyes—they were too tired to march all the way to ZelZaytun now. They would have to use these positions and get stuck camping there. At least there was a well nearby and Sanu could drink after sunset. Knowing he was close to Rattin provided some comfort as well.

24

JAB

Did you ever consider why the All-Planter chose poetry to communicate with us? Poems are easier to remember. Philosophers smarter than me think a different part of ourselves understands poetry. Children who stutter and seniors who forget both recite poetry to improve their speech. Poetry is not just beautiful, my friends; it's useful! In touching poetry, our souls get a glimpse of the All-Planter.

- Raticenna's lecture to schoolchildren

A breeze ruffled the hair atop Jab's head, exposed by the lack of headwraps. Knowing the same breeze stirred Kash's hair soothed the strange sensation. Macarona pulled a borrowed wagon cart with gardening tools, and the trio trudged toward ZelZaytun's outer gate. Jab hoped Kash wouldn't notice Jab's prayer rock, nestled in his clothes over his chest. He knew it didn't fit their disguise, but entering the holy city without it felt disrespectful to Mom.

Staring at his hindpaws without *looking like* he was averting his eyes from the holy tree proved difficult on the approach, but once they were near enough to the city, the city walls blessedly blocked the view of the Gnaverwood's trunk. He'd look at it once it was under Grovekeeper control.

Kash spoke from the side of his mouth. "Should we review our story?"

"No, I think I got it."

"Alright," Kash whispered. "Just remember, if you happen to say Ganan's name, immediately say 'Blest be Him.' But sound natural, like it's just part of his name. If you realize you didn't say it, don't add it as an afterthought. That would be *more* noticeable."

Jab nodded and sized up the guards. A porcupine and a beaver, armored and wearing surcoats with Lady Marjitay's coat of arms—the blasted crossbow and goose. Why anyone would want to follow someone with such ridiculous symbols was beyond him. Both guards stood with the curious polearms the defenders at the lake station used. The ends of the weapons resembled bird heads, warped and refashioned by a demonic spirit. If he ever got caught in a fight with a Sprouter soldier, he'd want to avoid that polearm at all costs. He'd seen the devastation they could cause already. His body wanted to tense, but he reminded himself that this would be a welcome sight for the parts they were playing.

As Macarona pulled the wagon closer, the two guards shifted, blocking the gate with their bodies. The beaver said something in Frenglese, and the porcupine echoed in their language. "State your business."

Kash released the reins. "Good day, friends. We're the gardeners requested by the Sapling."

The porcupine glared at them, then mumbled something to the beaver. After a quick back-and-forth between the guards, they raised their weapons. "The Sapling isn't expecting anyone," the porcupine said.

Jab bit down on his lip. This wasn't how things were supposed to go.

Kash cleared his throat. "Forgive me, sir knight, but we were requested some time ago. You see, we had to evade the enemy's troops and avoid the towns loyal to him. We must be weeks behind our expected arrival. The good Sapling has probably forgotten we were coming or assumed we weren't by this time. We came all the way from Banuj. I have the documents to prove we were requested. Allow me to get them."

Kash started rummaging through his sack. The lie came so easy, like a hyena finding a carcass, Jab wondered if Kash had lied about anything else, to him or to the Liberator. As quickly as it surfaced, Jab pushed the idea from his head. Kash was doing his job, nothing more.

The porcupine lowered his weapon and sighed. "The Sapling has... fallen ill. I'm afraid you cannot see him or his representatives."

Kash's weight shifted. Not good. Jab remembered him faltering the last time they encountered an armed porcupine.

"But we can't go back," Jab said. The eyes shifting to him suggested nobody expected or wanted him to talk. "Nasalid has even more troops surrounding the city now than when we crossed."

"Is that so?" The porcupine asked, eyebrow raised. "How close did you get to his camps?"

"Close enough I thought they'd hear us." Jab repressed a smile; everything he said was true.

Kash placed a paw around his shoulder. "Forgive my brother. This whole journey has been rough on him."

After another quick exchange between the two guards, the porcupine closed the distance between them. "What's that on your brother's chest?" He pointed at the lump on Jab's chest, the thin fabric covering his prayer rock.

Kash's whiskers stiffened. "I-I—"

"A gardening tool," Jab interjected. "Nasalid took our family's valuables and it's the only thing of value I have left." The lie came so easy.

"Heartless," the guard murmured. "You have my sympathy. So you have information about the enemy's camp? Could you approximate their numbers? Did you see their weapons?"

Jab nodded vigorously as if his prayer rock hadn't almost ruined their whole plan. "We saw much. We could tell the city's chief guard. Could you take us to him? And maybe after, we could visit the Sapling or a representative of his?"

Kash's paw dug into Jab's shoulder. Maybe he'd said too much.

Turning backward, the porcupine shouted a command in Frenglese, and the gate to ZelZaytun raised with a series of clicking *thunks*. The sound reminded Jab of crossbow gears turning; after so much target practice, he practically heard those *racka-clicks* in his sleep.

Another beaver plodded down from behind the gate, this one unarmored except for a helmet, yet his leather jerkin displayed a sewn-on patch: Lady Marjitay's coat of arms. He approached them and Macarona flinched. "We'll need to inspect your cart. Can't be too careful anymore."

"We understand, sir knight," Kash said. Before finally releasing Jab's shoulder, he squeezed, as if to say, "keep calm."

"Do either of you speak Frenglese?" the beaver inspector asked as he climbed up the back.

"No," Kash replied. "We are from the Sprouter community on the other side of the island. Banuj, south of here. Have you heard of our town?"

After saying something neutral sounding in Frenglese to the guards, the beaver slapped the back of the cart. "I haven't, but I also haven't gone much outside Olihort my whole life. Leave your cart here, and we'll deliver it to the Sapling for you. You two will meet the guard captain and tell him what you told me."

Jab and Kash hopped from the cart, and Kash fished a carrot from his pocket, which an eager Macarona chomped.

Heart racing, Jab's excitement made him forget Kash's warning. "Can you show us around the city? We've dreamed of seeing Olihort since we were kids." The city's false name felt putrid on his lips.

Kash pinched the bridge of his nose. "Please excuse my brother again. He's tired and we've been through a lot."

The beaver led them through the gate, and he glanced over his shoulder at them. "I bet you're both famished. Listen, we'll go straight to the captain. When we arrive, I'll tell his servants to prepare you lunch. On the way there, I'll point out the features of the city, places where Ganan preached, Blest Be Him."

All the fur on Jab's neck stiffened. They couldn't break the fast. Telling lies was one thing, but violating the fast felt so much worse.

Kash waved a paw. "After being out in the sun, I think we might get sick if we were to eat too soon. We've been so nervous about Nasalid that we haven't been able to sleep or eat much. We are hungry, but I'd hate to vomit or choke in front of your guard."

"Suit yourself. On our left, you'll see where Ganan, Blest Be Him, once congratulated the street cleaner on his faith."

Jab and Kash paused, allowing space for the beaver to speak. The stone city overflowed with history. Jab could dedicate the rest of his life to examining each stone and still only scratch the surface of their stories. For it was not only Ganan who trod these streets, but the Mulcher kings of old and the first Grovekeepers. Two brutal realities kept him from enjoying the tour: some stones had decades-old blood stains on them, and he couldn't visit the one thing he wanted to see more than anything else.

And even if he could, seeing the holy Gnaverwood up close would only be a painful reminder that his parents and brother could not advance to the afterlife while these Sprouters defiled it.

Their journey through the city wound through stone streets, and the power of the holiness moved him to wonder at the amazing things that had happened here. The myths felt more alive, more true. He glanced up at Kash, who was taking in the same sights, but didn't mirror Jab's reverence. Instead of marveling, he appeared to be calculating. Jab blinked hard. That's what he should've been doing too. This path, lined with vendors, was wide enough for four soldiers to walk abreast, maybe three mounted soldiers could pass, but definitely two.

An old woman in the nearest shop displayed rows of Sprouter prayer beads, not too different from his prayer rock, save their size and Ganan's rake on the end. Another merchant who could've been Rijat's age offered copies of the Sprouter holy book in what seemed like different languages. But the vendor who caught his eye next also caught his nose. A man, maybe Dad's age, sold sheltercake.

Sprouters ate that?

The aroma conjured memories of holidays and family time, events and nights he should've taken more effort to remember, never knowing his time with his parents and brother would end soon.

The aroma of sweet cheesy cake lingered in his nostrils, and the other vendors and stalls around them melted together in his mind.

When their beaver guide told them they were near the military quarter where they'd meet the guard captain, one last vendor stole Jab's attention.

A toy vendor. The dolls for sale were identical to Mutarra's. A lump formed in Jab's throat. Not only were there innocent rodents in this city, there were kids as well. He didn't see any playing in the street on their tour, but that dessert and those dolls proved it. Nasalid needed to know.

Passing the final vendor, the beaver waved to another guard who stood before an iron gate. The angular stonework around the gate and the design and cut of the iron bars suggested this was a Frenglese Sprouter addition to the city in the last few decades. It rose with a series of clanks, revealing a training arena and tight rows of squat buildings. An assortment of weapons lined the near wall, displaying swords, spears, and the horrific polearm. Squinting between the buildings, Jab found another gate on the opposite side. Possibly an additional exit for soldiers to make a counterattack to any besiegers. Nasalid needed to know that too.

"Ah, the captain is outside in the training yard," the beaver said, breaking Jab's trance. "He must have just returned from a scouting run." He called out something in Frenglese, and an armored porcupine turned around.

Betraying himself, Jab gasped.

It was the porcupine from before. The one who almost murdered them while they prayed. The one they lied to. The one who would know they had lied at the gate.

Zantiz.

A smirk twisted up the porcupine's snout. Zantiz said something to the beaver in Frenglese, and the iron gate behind them shut much faster than it opened. "So, my two desperate Sprouters have returned," he spoke in their language, at a volume and tone much smoother than what he'd just shouted. "Nasalid is not so clever as he seems. Discovered spies should be killed or reassigned."

"W-we're not spies," Kash said. "This is a misunderstanding."

Grabbing a polearm from the display, the porcupine approached them, and the beaver grabbed Jab and Kash's arms.

"There is no place in the Walled Garden for false Sprouters, but there is certainly room in the Droughtlands," the porcupine said. "Say 'hello' to DarkMouse down there. You'll get some company soon."

The polearm's curved shadow fell over Jab and Kash, blocking out the sun. Jab tapped the prayer rock over his chest, readying his final prayer.

25

SANU

*- General Ironseed's speech
before the Battle of Batina*

Under the desert sun, Sanu's dry mouth begged him to drink with the recuperating Sprouters, but he owed it to the All-Planter to exercise some willpower. Being spared the dishonorable battle, killing rodents lethargic from fasting, felt miraculous. Yet Nasalid's honor might be in question if the things Sanu heard about the attack on the lake depot were true—also killing rodents in their sleep. And cooking knights alive in their armor. Some hero. Sanu dreamed of glory, not this.

Seated between two abandoned tents, Sanu itched to return to ZelZaytun and get out of this heat, but each day brought the inevitable siege closer.

Nobody seemed to notice Sanu wasn't drinking or eating like the rest of the soldiers since he was beside Yagub, and every rodent maintained their distance from him.

Sir Brouglas approached the squirrels, whiskers drooping. "Yagub, my boy, you can't beat yourself up over getting tricked. Nasalid is clever."

Yagub nodded, and Sanu remembered how Jab acted the last time they played double siege together, making a sad confession that he'd lost.

"And you were probably hoping to see a real battle, Sanu." Brouglas said. Lips pursed, he switched languages. "See ... those techniques ... in action."

Shouting broke out behind them between the commanding officer and the seedling. One pointed toward ZelZaytun, and the other southeast. Strange, Sanu thought. Nothing was out that way.

Except Rattin.

Between the officer and seedling, an unarmored beaver who Sanu didn't recognize fidgeted. Unlike the garrison soldiers, this beaver's clothing bore the coat of arms of Lady Marjitay. If Sanu never saw that honking goose and crossbow ever again, he'd die a happy squirrel.

Sir Brouglas pointed a thumb over his shoulder at the newcomer. "Messenger from Olihort. They saw us coming and sent him ahead with orders from the Sapling."

Yagub's ears stiffened. "He's out of his confinement?"

"That's up for debate. See, the seedling is convinced that the message is from him, but the officer and I are not."

"What's the message say?" Sanu asked.

The beaver knight dropped his eyes, staring at the water flask in his paw. "There's a village loyal to Nasalid nearby. Orders came to attack it, to cut off his potential supplies."

More soldiers joined the growing huddle around the arguing officer and seedling.

Sanu's heart turned to stone. "Rattin. That's the village, isn't it?"

Yagub shot up. "That can't be true. The Sapling would never—"

Brouglas offered an apologetic smile. "I know. I said my piece, but I need both of you. You both understand the Sapling would never make this order."

"Will they want to listen to either of us?" Yagub's voice dripped with acid, but after a glance at Sanu, his tone softened. "I don't know how they'll treat Sanu if they know he's a Grovekeeper." He offered a kind smile. "I don't want you to have to pretend like you are something you're not or that you're not something you are. I'll lie for you. You'll stay protected that way. We can trust the Sapling and Cladh, but I don't know anyone else well enough to make that assumption."

Sanu peered at the arguing pair again, and a glint caught his eye. Light reflected off an amulet in the messenger's paw. The same one Cladh used. One that meant the holder was speaking with the Sapling's authority. Before Sanu could open his mouth, the seedling shouted, "Move out! We march on Rattin!"

Fists were raised, dropped weapons were grabbed, then the soldiers poured from the false camp, heading toward Sanu's childhood home.

Sanu clenched his fist. He'd find a way to save Rijat, Mutarra, and Qala, and anyone else in Rattin that he could. Sanu couldn't stop this battle, but he needed to at least try to save some lives. Jab once explained that the Divine Poetics had a line which went, "Saving one life is saving all rodentkind." Sanu had probably heard the line in the prayer house too, but it only stuck out to him because Jab had said it. As the other soldiers marched past, Sanu grabbed Yagub's wrist.

"You both know this is wrong," Sanu said. "Help me ride out ahead and warn the townsrodents."

"Let's go." Yagub hopped onto Vermitch and offered a paw to help Sanu join him.

"You're crazy, Yagub." The steel in Brouglas' eyes made Sanu pause. That wasn't like him. "They'll shoot you down with a crossbow if they see you ride out ahead. You want to kill Sanu and my horse along with yourself?" He exhaled, releasing some tension in his shoulders, which made his armor squeak. "Ride alongside them, then when they split up to start fighting, run along to find whoever you can save or warn. Break off too soon and they'll figure out what you're doing and stop you."

"No," Yagub said.

Sir Brouglas scowled. "I'm your knight, and you're my squire. I've loved you like a brother. You won't throw your life away, and that's an order." In a flash, he reached up and snatched Vermitch's reins. "By Ganan's Blisters, I will drag you back to Olihort if I have to."

The last soldier stormed past them.

Yagub sighed, mumbled an apology to Sanu, then slid off the saddle. Brouglas put his paws on Yagub's shoulders and the two men stared at each other, eyes full of anger and regret.

And Sanu knew what *he'd* regret. While they were distracted, he grabbed the reins and kicked Vermitch, taking off at a gallop behind the running soldiers.

Brouglas and Yagub shouted for Sanu to turn around, but Sanu didn't care. Not when innocent rodents were at risk. He wasn't about to sit back while Rattin burned. He'd already helplessly watched his parents succumb to fever and his brother fall to his death. The past was out of his control, but this wasn't. Maybe he could make a wide circle and slip around the soldiers unnoticed.

He raced ahead, and the over thousand-strong force closed on Rattin. The horns came into view, the site of the earlier massacre that stole Jab from him. Passing the soldiers in the formation's rear, Sanu wondered how many had revenge on their mind. How many of their friends were in that group of knights killed on Rattin's horns, and how many of them were killed when Nasalid took the lake depot. Or were they only motivated by protecting the city that was sacred to them?

He couldn't know their intentions, but he knew his: he must be a protector.

Pushing Vermitch harder, he reached the halfway point of the rushing soldiers. Rattin's homes and prayer house came into view. The soldiers were breathing hard. Running in armor under the afternoon sun must have been punishing. One soldier near the side of the column lifted his helmet and vomited, gasping. A comrade shoved him aside, letting him fall into the grass.

Perhaps the officer and seedling urging the soldiers to run and fight in the heat and their armor were the cruel ones here. Sanu felt bad for him but pressed forward. At least that was one less Sprouter who might take a Grovekeeper's life today.

Two more soldiers broke ranks to vomit.

Then ten.

If Sanu weren't clutching Vermitch's reins, urging the horse forward, he might've scratched his head. Maybe some camp fever was going around. Dad had told him stories about how sickness took more lives than spears, but it just sounded like a parental admonishment to wash more.

Now he had to wonder. In his time with the Sprouters, Sanu noticed they didn't clean themselves often compared to Grovekeepers and Mulchers. Maybe their poor hygiene was dooming them—Jab would've said the power of prayer really did ward off demons, in part because of the washing.

Another five broke to lose their lunches.

Rattin was close now. Anybody standing on a rooftop looking in their direction would see the approaching horde.

But anyone on a roof wouldn't face their direction now: prayer time approached, judging by the sun's position.

Sanu's eyes widened. They'd descend on the town while everyone was stopping to pray and feeling lethargic from the heat and fasting. Maybe Nasalid would come to the rescue, hopefully not with fire and hopefully more mercifully than whatever he did at the lake depot.

As Sanu approached the front of the horde, more soldiers peeled off to barf. If the people of Rattin couldn't hear the marching soldiers' hindpaws, they might hear the chorus of vomiting.

The commanding officer stopped and vomited, along with the seedling at the front, hunched over and hurling.

Soon the whole garrison clambered to a fumbling fall, most of them puking and the others comforting their comrades-in-arms.

Easing on Vermitch, Sanu stared open-mouthed at the heaving soldiers. If some fever were coursing through them, Sanu should've felt something himself. He knew philosophers and doctors debated how sickness spread, but one thing was sure: most sicknesses came from other rodents.

He'd been in the midst of them for two weeks and didn't have many chances to wash himself the last few days.

Unless they weren't sick. Injuries could cause sickness and weren't contagious.

And the same could be said for poison.

Sanu halted Vermitch in front of the commanding officer and hoped his Frenglese was clear. "Retreat to Olihort! Something is wrong."

After a vomit so intense it bordered on exercise, the hamster wiped his chin, peering up at Sanu with sunken eyes. "We kn-know."

The seedling let loose a furious puke and snarled. "Nasalid poisoned us. That squirrel from Olihort led us to the fake camp. The well was meant for us. We have to turn around and regroup." An orchestra of heaving soldiers muffled the seedling's shouts.

Sanu nodded. "It seems like he did. Let's get everyone to Olihort. They have healers inside. You can't stay out here in the open."

The truth stung. A kid from ZelZaytun or Rattin could've wandered over to that well for a drink.

"The water of that town and Olihort may be poisoned too." Sanu guided Vermitch away from the officer and seedling. "I'll warn the townsrodents about Nasalid's treachery. They'll never support him if they know the truth." To think the jird he'd once considered a hero could stoop so low made Sanu seethe.

"Ganan's Speed to you," the officer said.

"Blest Be Him," the seedling added. "That boy is the savior of Rattin."

26

JAB

- Divine Poetics

Jab had dreamed of *living* in ZelZaytun, not dying here. The Gnaverwood's shadow was supposed to be a cooling embrace, not a burial shroud, yet here Jab was, restrained by an enemy.

Sir Zantiz's devilbeak descended on Kash. Jab struggled in the beaver's restraining grip as it passed over him, but he couldn't squirm out.

With a flick, Jab latched his tail onto Kash's wrist, desperate to pull him out of the way, but he moved too slow.

"Kash!" Jab shouted.

Kash had his whole life ahead of him. He didn't deserve this. The beakish polearm descended. "Please, no!"

The porcupine wheeled on Jab as Kash fell to the ground. The *thud* of his limp body seemed to reverberate; a moment too horrific to last only one second.

"Ready to talk?" Zantiz's voice remained calm, breathing only slightly faster.

"Never," Jab hissed.

The beaver restraining Jab loosened his grip, rubbing blood off his face with his shoulder.

Weapon raised, Zantiz swung for another strike, but Jab watched these swings at the lake and knew how it would fall. He twisted out of the soldier's looser grip, leapt to the left, and the weapon sliced the air in front of the beaver's muzzle.

Jab glimpsed Kash's slouched corpse. He deserved better than to die here, but Jab couldn't stop to mourn. The porcupine swung again, and Jab ducked low, sidestepping to his right.

Grunting, the beaver unsheathed a longsword and charged toward Jab. Jab sprinted toward the training arena, grabbing a sword with his tail. The design was the Frenglese one-pawed straight variety, the kind that could stab or slash, but would fare poorly against cavalry. No wonder they couldn't conquer the rest of the island with weapons like this. Jab tossed the weapon into his paw. He could never defend himself against these two, but all he needed was a distraction. The gate to the rest of the city was still open.

Seeing where Jab's eyeline went, the porcupine shouted something in Frenglese, and the gate began closing. It took twelve *clinks* to open, so he had only a few seconds.

Clink-clink. Thunk.

The porcupine and beaver stood shoulder-to-shoulder, blocking the gate. Jab charged. He had one chance.

Clink-clink. Thunk.

Jab threw the sword at the beaver. The improvised projectile would never connect, but it didn't need to because he flinched and backed away.

Clink-clink. Thunk.

Smirking, Zantiz rotated the polearm to the spiked side, and thrust it like a spear. Jab banked left.

Clink-clink. Thunk.

As the spear whooshed past him, pushing a gust of air through his fur, Jab used his tail to parry. He wasn't strong enough to disarm the porcupine or pull him to the ground, but he only needed a simple redirect.

Clink-clink. Thunk.

Free from his attackers, Jab darted toward the gate and rolled under the closing portcullis.

Clink-clink. Thunk.

An iron gate separated him from his attackers. Jab was safe for now, but the beaver and porcupine called out something in unison. Jab had no clue what the words were, but he assumed they meant, "stop that squirrel."

The townsrodents stopped haggling in the marketplace and turned on Jab. A young kid screamed. Jab probably had splatters of Kash's blood on him.

If Sanu were here, he'd swoop in heroically and swing his scimitar to keep everyone away, but all Jab had was the little self-defense dagger. Jab jumped atop a merchant's cart, then used his momentum to get behind a shop. He undid his vest, turned it inside out, then banked toward the sheltercake baker's stall. Bakers kept water, solvents, and powdered spices, which could remove his friend's blood and dye his fur in a pinch.

Clamors in the street rose and echoed, surely calling for Jab's arrest and apprehension, maybe even death.

Nasalid had to know about the innocent rodents in ZelZaytun. This information would change his whole battle strategy.

Jab sprinted between shops, overturning baskets and hopping around passersby until his snout led him to the bakery. Even though he was behind the line of vendors, the aroma was unmistakable. He opened the back door to a kitchen. The shopkeeper was occupied in the front, and Jab slowed to a crawl until he found the cinnamon; he couldn't risk unnecessary noise. A stone jar of water sat beside the oven. This was clearly meant to put out a fire, so Jab knew he wouldn't ruin any food by using it to wash the blood out.

The baker's voice echoed, and Jab sank behind the oven. His palms sweated so much he could've washed himself without the jar of water. He strained his ears. The baker's accent wasn't too different from his, but he spoke Frenglese.

The calm, yet winded voice responding to the baker was unmistakable.

Zantiz.

Jab wished he knew Frenglese. Sanu was the one always trying to learn a few words from the traders when they passed through town, which Jab had always found pointless.

Whatever words passed between baker and soldier ended.

After counting to five and catching his breath, Jab left cover and grabbed a pawful of powdered cinnamon. Quietly, he slapped it onto himself. With his inside-out vest and the confectionary camouflage making his brown fur darker, he had a rudimentary disguise. He pulled out his coin—pay from Nasalid—and left it in the middle of the floor, then ducked out into the back alley. They would be expecting him to escape ZelZaytun, so for now, the safest direction to go was toward where Kash was murdered.

Soldiers marched by.

They passed him, and Jab breathed a sigh.

He'd evaded escape but was stuck in a hostile city. The likelihood of the city going on lockdown had increased dramatically. That porcupine from the Droughtlands was hunting him. Jab's stomach roared. He'd overexerted himself on a day when he'd been fasting. The pangs pushed him, tempting him to break the fast and find a snack, but knowing he'd escaped that murderer brought him a measure of strength and confidence.

Which melted away when he realized he'd need to tell Nasalid that his favorite scout, not to mention the last person who felt like family to Jab, had died. If Jab survived to tell him, of course.

His only hope lay in finding a caravan or wagon leaving the city and hiding in its cargo, which would be challenging, considering the cargoes came to the city laden and left empty. Yet he had to find a way. He owed it to Kash, Sanu, and his parents.

"Young man." He recognized the voice and accent.

Heart racing, Jab whipped around. A gerbil with graying fur and a puff of powdered cinnamon near his paws greeted him. The baker.

Smiling, he produced a coin. "You overpaid for the materials you took. I'm a fair businessrodent."

Jab's mouth dried. No words formed.

"Please, take a breath, friend. Let's head back to the bakery."

Jab followed the gerbil back to the bakery, this time entering through the front. Pleasant aromas wafted around, yet Jab was too stiff to enjoy them.

"Would you like to pray together? It's midday."

Jab stared, slack jawed.

The baker flashed a wooden sign which read "come back soon" and another line underneath in Frenglese. He displayed it in the doorframe, then beckoned Jab to follow him into the kitchen.

"I can imagine you're confused," the gerbil said. "There are very few of us in ZelZaytun. My parents and a few others became Sprouters to earn some mercy from the conquerors, but they continued their practice at home and raised me Grovekeeper. I am unsure if the All-Planter will judge us kindly for this on Pruning Day, but times were desperate. I knew selling sheltercake would one day attract a true Grovekeeper." He winked, then gestured at the powder in Jab's fur. "But I had always assumed they'd come through the front door." He pointed to Jab's chest. "I also assumed they would hide their prayer rocks better."

Jab fussed with the rock. Kash would've laughed at another Grovekeeper seeing through their disguise.

The baker opened a locked cabinet and pulled out a prayer rug. "You may use mine." He hobbled over to a wash basin, and did all the ritual cleaning of his paws, hindpaws, and face. After taking the few minutes for prayer, he gestured for Jab to do the same.

When Jab finished praying, tears streaked his fur, mixing with the powder and last bits of dried blood, washing away in the basin. "Thank you, kind sir. Do you have somewhere safe to go?"

"So, the rumors are true. Nasalid the Liberator means to retake the city? I hear the soldiers murmuring about it. The captain of the guard found out about our month of fasting, so he is sure the attack will happen when it's over."

Kash and Sanu would probably admonish Jab for revealing so much to a stranger or trusting anything he said. "I'm a scout, but my leader was captured and killed."

"Ah, you have my condolences. May he find the All-Planter's favor on Pruning Day."

"I hope so," Jab said. "But I need to leave the city. Tell Nasalid what I saw. He needs to know about you and the others. He has an advisor and a lieutenant who would want to destroy the city and kill everyone inside."

The baker gerbil stroked his wispy beard. "I should hope Nasalid would follow the practices of battle and war set forth in the Divine Poetics. And yet some part of me doesn't. General Ironseed tried, and he ultimately failed. But you must get your information to him. I have a way out of the city. A friend of mine is a rug merchant, and he has a delivery leaving the city. He sewed a massive rake into the design of new rugs, and they are being sold back in the islands of Freng. I'll sneak you into a rug, and you can leave the wagon once it passes the gates. You will have to go the long way around the outside of the city though. The roads to Rattin and the lake depot have been closed off to travel."

"Thank you," Jab said. "I'll tell Nasalid about your kindness."

"The All-Planter knows, and that's what matters. I'll send you off with some bread for when you break the fast tonight. His shipment should be leaving soon. I can give you one more piece of information to give to Nasalid. The Sapling and Lady Marjitay share power here. I don't understand how, but they do, and it's icy. The Sapling is reasonable, but the so-called Goose of Olihort is... She lives up to her name. Now, let's get to the wagon."

At least hiding in a wagon meant he could avert his eyes from the holy Gnaverwood, but it would also mean that the driver could take him back to the dreaded porcupine. Jab's trust was about to either be rewarded or punished.

27

SANU

Vermitch whinnied as Sanu brought them to a halt outside Rattin. The townsrodents should've finished their prayers by now, yet the town lacked bustle and movement. No giggling kids or haggling adults. No sounds echoing from the prayer house. Sanu guided Vermitch onto the main road; the town was deserted. He peeked in windows. Nothing.

Maybe Nasalid descended on the town, killing everyone like at the lake depot. They'd killed everyone, so nobody could help the

Sprouters. Sanu's nostrils flared at the thought, as he searched for signs of struggle. He hopped off Vermitch, anchoring with his tail, and patted the horse's neck.

Sanu entered Rijat's home, the house that would've been his and Jab's if it weren't for Nasalid the invader.

"Rijat?" Sanu whispered.

Nothing.

"Qala?" Sanu asked the emptiness.

Louder, he called, "Mutarra?"

Nothing.

If Nasalid's troops had torn through and killed everyone, there should've been blood, clumps of fur, or overturned chairs. Nothing. The house seemed pristine.

Sanu poked his snout into the back room. The whole home was bare and tidy.

Sanu tried the neighbor's home. Then the sheltercake bakery. Then the prayer house.

Nothing, nothing, and nothing. Nobody was here and nothing sat out of place. Everyone left, and by the looks of it, willingly and not in a hurry.

They either fled into the countryside, joined Nasalid willingly, or maybe were accepted into ZelZaytun on a liberated Sapling's order.

His heart lightened at the final prospect, but as he rejoined Vermitch in the middle of the road, he was forced to see Lady Marjitay's coat of arms again on the saddle. There was no way that honking goose of a mole rat would allow the villagers of Rattin into ZelZaytun.

The Sprouters weren't all kind like the Sapling and Brouglas, and they also weren't all like Lady

Marjitay. Just as the evil emissary couldn't represent all Grovekeepers.

If Nasalid knew this, maybe this siege would go differently.

Sanu would stop this from happening.

Nasalid's camp couldn't be too far from Rattin if they could attack the horns and the lake depot. Logic suggested his camp sat somewhere between those three points. The town, the hills, and the lake.

He knew where he'd start. Tail assisting him, he climbed onto Vermitch. Sitting atop the horse gave him a wider vantage point, and he turned the borrowed steed to face the sacred city.

At this hottest time of the day toward the end of the month of fasting, there couldn't be much activity in Nasalid's camp, which would allow him to slip in unnoticed.

Cantering forward, a peculiar object caught his attention. To one side, a tall piece of lumber poked over a thicket of trees.

This wooden object was a triangular shape and stood taller than two trees. Then, a wooden arm rose up from the bottom of it, swinging forward in a big *whoosh*.

It threw a boulder toward ZelZaytun's walls, landing with a crash that could have woken the dead. Sanu's heart caught in his throat. The Sprouter soldiers knew good Grovekeepers would be fasting and less energetic today. They weren't expecting an attack.

It seemed like Nasalid was having his troops break the fast so they could start fighting today when the Sprouters weren't ready. Sanu didn't have time to go find the general, not when ZelZaytun's orphans sat undefended.

As another boulder flew toward the city walls, Sanu urged the nervous Vermitch forward. Stone walls fractured and crumbled. Once there was an opening in the wall, troops would follow.

The garrison meant to bolster the city's defenses were still puking in the field and on the wrong side of the city.

A third boulder crashed into the wall, and ZelZaytun's gates shook. Another gallop brought him close enough to hear soldiers' screams puncturing the afternoon air.

But Sanu had to protect those orphans, no matter what. Those were innocent kids, and this conflict had ruined enough lives already.

The gate clinked open as Sanu approached—somebody must've seen Lady Marjitay's colors on Vermitch. They'd be disappointed to learn about their reinforcements spilling their insides in the grass outside.

Vermitch stiffened under Sanu, and he wondered if the horse feared entering the city, closer to the weakening walls, closer to the source of the vibrations that must be shaking Vermitch's hooves by now.

Pulling up the hill into ZelZaytun and approaching the gate, Sanu shouted, "The reinforcements from Kraksnout are delayed! Protect the children!"

He passed under the gate, which clinked behind him. By the expressions on these rodents' faces, they'd rather guard a gate than tend to the growing hole in their defenses. They didn't want to face Nasalid's forces.

Sanu gulped as he rode past. Maybe Nasalid would spare these cowards, let them return to Freng or live here peacefully if they'd surrender; hopefully the whole city would. The fortifications around the gate seemed so pointless against such a massive siege engine. Nasalid must have some of the finest engineering minds.

Alarm bells rang throughout the city, and screaming rodents tore through the streets, slamming doors behind them or pounding on closed doors.

This was the old residential quarter. Hopefully, a safe place.

Sanu and Vermitch clopped through the alleys, and reached the end of the residential quarter, where a wide opening between the buildings let Sanu get his bearings. The Gnaverwood grove was on his right, an incongruous symbol of love and protection over a city that wars were fought over.

To his left, a crumbling city wall. Sanu's stomach roared and his dry throat reminded him that he didn't have much spare energy. He urged Vermitch forward, toward the Sapling's Gananhall.

In his periphery, he saw the inner wall shatter, allowing more light and dust to pour into the city.

Grovekeeper soldiers cheered over the rubble. As the cheering grew over the crash of fracturing stone, a chanted word became clear. "Na-sa-lid!" they chanted. It should've been a relief.

But soldiers willing to break the fast might also be depraved enough to kill innocent people who got in their way.

Or loot and pillage for gold and valuables.

As Sanu raced toward the Gananhall, he passed a squirrel kid with cinnamon-colored fur by an overturned cart, spilling out loose rugs. If it weren't for the fur color, Sanu would've almost thought he looked like Jab.

Maybe Sanu would fight another Grovekeeper today, a trained soldier who could cut him to pieces in seconds. Or maybe a neighbor. Perhaps Rijat had traded his carpentry tools for a scimitar and would cut him down.

Sanu had to trust the stories of Nasalid's nobility were not only true but also extended to his troops. Judging by that evil emissary who burned Sprouter holy objects, that felt unlikely.

Soon the Gananhall's tall rake cast a shadow over horse and rider. Sanu readied his scimitar.

Shrieking Sprouters of various species scurried through the street in front of him, desperate to find shelter.

Nasalid's cheering troops grew louder behind him. "Na-sa-lid! Na-sa-lid! Na-sa-lid!" It was a name he chanted as a kid. But if they were approaching behind him, their goal wasn't to destroy the grove. That left either Lady Marjitay or the Sapling.

Rounding the front of the Gananhall, Sanu dismounted from the exhausted Vermitch. The poor guy had been through too much today.

"Na-sa-lid! Na-sa-lid!"

Scimitar in paw, Sanu stood with his back to the Gananhall entrance. He'd defend those orphans inside or die trying.

28

JAB

My father had two friends whom I called "Uncle." One was a traditional Mulcher and the other a devout Sprouter. They were glassblowers. When the Sprouters invaded from Freng, my Sprouter Uncle hid my father and my Mulcher Uncle. Our families survived because of his kindness. I believe the All-Planter will reunite those three friends in the hereafter.

- Raticenna's Collected Sermons

Jab stepped into the wagon, finding a fold in the rugs he could hide in. The wagon shook, complicating his attempt.

ZelZaytun shook, rattling the wagon along with it. A violent rumble made Jab smack his face against the wagon, lodging his prayer rock into his fur.

Gasping, Jab peered up at the city's crumbling inner wall. Rocks bigger than houses rained from the sky.

A shattered boulder ransacked the street, bringing debris and pulverized stone with it.

The siege had begun. Nasalid had no idea there were innocent rodents in here. Or worse, he knew and didn't care.

Jab shouted at the driver. "Run! Find a safe place to hide with your donkey." Finding Nasalid was more important than ever, and the widening hole in the wall suggested a direct path.

Another boulder thudded through, closer to the ground and more intact than the first. The driver unhitched his donkey and they moved.

Jab shielded himself from the rubble, putting his forearms in front of his eyes. The boulder rolling into the street matched the same general shape of his prayer rock, which was as cruel as Nasalid attacking the holy city during the month of fasting.

Jab climbed atop the wagon and grabbed a small rug. He unrolled it, stretching it over himself. It would block any debris speeding toward his face.

As he readied his makeshift shield, a squirrel atop a horse galloped past him. The rider looked short, too young to be a soldier, and the horse sported Lady Marjitay's garish coat of arms. Hopefully this kid was on his way to beg her to surrender.

A third boulder crashed into the walls, and Jab readied his rug shield, then ran toward the crumbling wall.

He had to find a soldier. Tell them what Nasalid would want. Avoid the innocents. Just go straight for Lady Marjitay.

A chorus broke out over the cracking stone and crumbling walls.

"Na-sa-lid!" They were chanting as if the city had already surrendered.

A gaggle of exhausted-looking Sprouter soldiers approached. The ones in armor seemed like they were limping and the ones without any looked like they'd deprived themselves of more food and water than a Grovekeeper mid-fast.

This would be a slaughter.

A group of Nasalid's infantry split off to face the attackers, and Jab climbed a wooden pillar supporting a fabric canopy. From his new vantage point, he scanned the splintering crowd of soldiers for an officer.

Two feathers on a red-streaked helmet. *Thank the All-Planter!* An officer.

Jab bounded off the roof, shedding his disguise and adorning his concealed headwraps.

Approaching the Grovekeeper troops, he called over the shouting, "I'm a scout! I'm Nasalid's scout!"

Soldiers trickled between houses, splitting off toward the different quarters of the city. One soldier, a gerbil, noticed Jab and stopped.

"I'm a scout," Jab said. "I was stuck in the city before I could give my report to the Liberator." He thought his heart would jump through his throat.

The gerbil's eyes widened. "What'd you find?"

"There are innocents here!"

The soldier's jaw dropped. "The Liberator needs to know. Let's get my commander." The gerbil grabbed Jab's wrist, dragging him against the flow of on-rushing soldiers.

They stopped in front of the officer Jab spied and relayed the message. The officer screamed to the troops, "Watch for innocents! Children and Grovekeepers are here."

As loud as Jab had been, and as much more forceful this officer was, it might as well have been the sound of a pin dropping in the noise of battle. They needed to get to a war drummer or horn blower.

"Sir!" the gerbil cried as they broke through the fray.

A jerboa turned around, wearing the three-feathered helmet of a lieutenant. Jorjim. The mace affixed to his tail gleamed in the afternoon sun, freshly polished and ready for battle.

Jab yearned to rub his prayer rock and desperately ask the All-Planter to let him wake from this nightmare.

"Who is this?" the lieutenant asked.

"H-he's one of our scouts," the soldier replied. "He has news for the Liberator. There are innocents here."

A scowl crept across Jorjim's snout. "No, he's not, and no, there aren't. All the scouts reported in before the siege commenced. You found a street urchin. A Sprouter spy."

Jab's skin crawled. Jorjim lied to his soldier because he didn't want Jab to stop the slaughter.

Jab did nothing to stop his parents, Sanu, or Kash from dying. He was done being a helpless bystander while others got hurt. He'd rather go to the Droughtlands than let any more innocents die. "Traitor! Liar!" Jab hissed. "You'll never bring back our dead with revenge."

The soldier gazed between Jab and Jorjim as cries of fighting roared behind them. His grip on Jab's wrist stayed firm.

"Kill the spy," Jorjim said. "He's trying to trick you."

"S-sir?" the gerbil asked. His grip tightened.

Scowl melting into stony neutrality, the lieutenant tapped his tail-mace into the street, kicking up dust and rubble. "You heard me, soldier."

The last crowd of soldiers poured into the city behind them.

Nobody nearby was watching.

"N-no." Some composure returning, the soldier released Jab and pushed him out of the way. "Jorjim, I won't kill a—*hrrk!*"

Thud.

The soldier fell to his knees as Jorjim's mace crushed his chest.

Two deaths today.

Before Jab could react, Jorjim swatted Jab's chest with his mace.

Crack!

The sound came from Jab's prayer rock, held fast over his heart, where Mom always told him to keep it. It shattered into dust in his clothes as Jab rolled to the ground.

Jab scampered away, not bothering to wipe the blood off his fur or nurse his bruised chest.

"Get back here!" Jorjim roared, thumping behind him.

Jab hopped across the chunks of destroyed wall, sprinting and jumping. The murder weapon slowed down his pursuer.

A troop of engineers rushed forward across the field, carrying a series of planks toward the debris, visible through the outermost portion of the destroyed wall. It would create a makeshift road for Nasalid's cavalry to pour into the city.

And maybe among those engineers, somebody would recognize Jab. He just had to get to them.

Whoosh!

A heavy tail swung in front of Jab, stopping his advance.

With the speed of hatred and revenge pushing him, Jorjim had him cornered among the rubble, blocking the only escape.

Jab half-knelt, discreetly grabbing a pawful of gravel and shattered rock. "I'm sorry. I surrender."

"Meet the Sprouters in the Droughtlands." Heartless words from a heartless jerboa. With a heave, the tail-mace came down, rushing toward Jab's head.

In one motion, Jab rose, threw the debris into Jorjim's eyes, and spun away.

Cursing and pawing at his eyes, Jorjim's tail crashed into a pile of loose stones.

With both paws, Jab grabbed the largest stone and heaved it onto the jerboa's tail.

The lieutenant yelped, but Jab pushed away any guilt from his mind, since a broken tail would heal.

Jorjim snarled. "I'll kill you and every Sprouter on this island."

Sanu would've quipped back, but Jab chose his own path. "I forgive you. If you continue to fight, I hope it's for the right reasons."

More clangs of metal on metal echoed nearby. These soldiers needed to know about the innocents as much as Nasalid, and yet the only one who could call them off was writhing and cursing in rubble.

Tempting fate, Jab bounced toward Jorjim and grabbed his helmet. Jab wasn't as tall as the lieutenant, but his tail could help for a quick illusion.

"Give me that!" Jorjim called, wincing as he struggled with his trapped tail.

"You don't deserve it," Jab muttered as he wiggled it free.

The rubble of what was once ZelZaytun's mighty walls spread out into the street with shattered stones of various sizes. Jab hopped onto one, then another, until he was high enough to hop onto a rooftop. Below to the right, Sprouter fighters were surrounded by Nasalid's troops. Below to the left, another group of Grovekeepers advanced toward the residential quarter.

Once there was a lull in the noise, Jab rotated his helmeted tail tip toward them and shouted. "Hey! Turn around! There are children here! Press toward the palace and ignore the homes!" To impersonate Jorjim, Jab added so much gravel to his voice that he thought he'd either puke his guts out or cough up a lung. "Go ahead and I'll join you!" Maybe he'd puke up a lung or cough up his guts. Maimon would know some good remedies.

Behind him, the engineer corps with their rolling planks arrived at the destroyed wall, and Jab recognized Nasalid's honor guard.

The Liberator himself was here.

Jab's hair stood on end. The engineer crew laid their planks over Jorjim—from their vantage point, they couldn't see him in the rubble. The mounted soldiers would gallop over him. Steeling himself, Jab said a prayer that the lieutenant would live, so he could stand trial for a court-martial. Jab bounded toward the approaching general.

It was time for him to know the truth.

29

SANU

Sanu wondered about the boy he passed in the street on the way to the Gananhall. Seeing a squirrel his age was a painful reminder of Jab, but also a sign that he needed to defend the city's innocents.

Vermitch whinnied beside Sanu, and he urged the horse to stand behind him in the Gananhall's entrance. The poor horse must be worried about Brouglas and Yagub.

He gripped his scimitar tight, and shouts of battle erupted behind the building, approaching. Thudding hindpaws came up the street in front of him. Sanu would be boxed in soon. It couldn't end like this; there were innocent rodents who had homes to go back to in Rattin, and orphaned kids in danger here. They were him and he was them. Brouglas had saved him from the fire, and Sanu needed to save these orphans from the chaos of battle.

From the palace quarters, a garrison emerged, led by Zantiz brandishing a devilbeak. When the soldiers arrived at the Gananhall, Zantiz stooped in front of Sanu. "Protecting the Sapling, eh?"

"N-no. The orphans inside." Sanu inched backward.

"Nasalid will loot this place. You know that, right? I'm here to get my men out for the fight." Zantiz motioned for his nearest soldier. "You, go tell the guards in there we need them to help repel the heathens."

The ordered soldier brushed past Sanu, shoving him aside. Sanu's grip on his scimitar loosened. How could he possibly think to defend such a place against real soldiers, if a glorified bodyguard to Lady Marjitay could shove him aside so easily? Vermitch proved more of an obstacle for the soldier than Sanu.

Hooves clambered up the street.

Sanu's heart raced, and Vermitch stomped.

"Get in formation, vermin!" Zantiz's detachment of troops, about twenty total, staggered out, devilbeaks extended. They occupied the width of the street, and any attackers would have to go through them. A thin line for sure, but Sanu knew their armor's strength and how dangerous the devilbeaks were.

Zantiz called the order but remained beside Sanu. The soldier who'd entered the Gananhall returned with five more guards. That meant Cladh and the Sapling were now unprotected, but also no longer under imprisonment. At Zantiz's command, the other guards joined the formation.

Nasalid's mounted troops roared through the street, but halted in front of Zantiz's troops. An order came out and the mounted soldiers pulled back, replaced by mounted archers. They rained down arrow fire, which plinked off the Frenglese armor. Arrows bounced like raindrops, clattering into the street.

"Advance!" Zantiz called. The garrison marched a step forward, but Zantiz remained beside Sanu.

Whoever commanded Nasalid's troops shouted, "Again!"

More arrows descended. None of Zantiz's rodents flinched, broke ranks, or fell, but a few sported new dents in their armor.

"Fools," Zantiz muttered through a chuckle. "Advance!"

Arrows rained again.

As his garrison took another step forward, the lead rodent lost his footing, tripping over a fallen arrow. The second he did, two of Nasalid's soldiers ran forward and grabbed his devilbeak.

Zantiz's other soldiers scrambled to protect their comrade, but they also tripped or stumbled over the arrows littering the street, and Nasalid's troops overtook the garrison.

Their heavy armor lost its advantage when they were slipping and falling on their backs.

The last of Lady Marjitay's defenders had fallen.

Except for Zantiz himself.

Nasalid's horde bouldered toward the Gananhall, and Zantiz pushed Sanu backward into Vermitch. Zantiz spun around, wielding his devilbeak, hate in his eyes. Sanu hated himself for once thinking this guy had good intentions.

A mounted soldier charged Zantiz with a spear, and the porcupine drove his polearm through the horse's neck. Vermitch whinnied, and the other soldiers gave Zantiz a wide berth. Sanu wanted to shout at Zantiz for his unnecessary cruelty, but no words formed.

Another rider, this one unarmed, pushed through to the front. After a blink and eye rub, Sanu recognized him.

Difatim.

The jerboa emissary, the one who insulted the whole city of ZelZaytun and every Sprouter in it. His leading troops would end poorly.

Difatim smirked, staring down his horse at Zantiz. "Ah, the obstinate porcupine. So you guard your Gananhall, hoping to spare it from our looters? Is Lady Marjitay hiding in there? Bring her to me."

Zantiz switched his stance to hold the devil-beak in one paw, then turned around and pulled Sanu in front of him.

"This boy is a Grovekeeper," Zantiz said. "One step forward by any of your rodents and I kill him."

Sanu's fury made him want to scream.

Cocking his head, the noble jerboa appraised Sanu as if he was a melon. "He's a boy. One life is meaningless." A few of the other soldiers shot Difatim dirty looks at the comment.

"And how many lives will you throw away to get to me?" Zantiz taunted. "Besides, you'll want this boy in particular. He gave me valuable secrets about Grovekeepers. I already sent those back to Freng. You think Nasalid can keep this city? Every prince on those islands will band together and rip this city apart with the information I got from him. The All-Planter wants us here."

Those questions Zantiz had asked about Grovekeepers. He wasn't honestly curious about his neighbors but mining Sanu for ways to exploit them. Sanu couldn't believe what an idiot he was.

"You can kill the boy, for all I care." Difatim's cold voice chilled Sanu.

Zantiz pressed the devilbeak's hook against Sanu's neck. This evil noble wouldn't protect Cladh or the Sapling.

Sanu leaned his neck away from the weapon and called out, "I have a better offer! Arrest him and find the Sapling inside. He has the authority to surrender. The troops will listen to—"

Whack!

The strike came fast, making the air whistle around it.

An arrow went through Zantiz's face.

The monster of a porcupine lost his grip on Sanu, who sidestepped the collapsing corpse.

Difatim approached Sanu. "Their Sapling is inside? How about the riches?" By the indifference in his voice, it seemed Difatim must not have remembered Sanu from the farce of a negotiation last month.

"You can't take any of the holy things from there." Rage bubbled in Sanu. "There are children inside. Innocent—"

Fast as a striking viper, the noble clasped his paw over Sanu's mouth. He turned to the troops. "Enter the Gananhall. Take everything gold, all the artwork, and any valuables you can find. Remember, I made you rich. Bring the Sapling to me. Kill anyone else."

After exchanging nervous glances with each other, some of the soldiers nodded and jogged inside. One slowed as he passed, staring with a raised eyebrow at Difatim and Sanu. Another pulled Vermitch by the reins, satisfied with this prize.

Hunching over Sanu, the jerboa came so close to his face that his breath tickled Sanu's whiskers. "If you really were a Grovekeeper, you'd understand there are no innocent rodents with Frenglese blood. They're all part of the massacre of our ancestors. They stole our holy land. Destroying them will bring rodents of the true faith together. You must see that."

Sanu still had his scimitar behind his back.

This wasn't a trained soldier, but a pampered noble who'd been gifted a commanding office. Probably a concession Nasalid had to make to garner some important family's support. Maybe Sanu had a chance against him.

Using his tail, Sanu raised his scimitar and pointed it at the jerboa's face. The noble backed away. "Don't be hasty, boy."

The soldier who'd taken Vermitch ran over. "What's going on?"

Sanu shot pleading eyes to the soldier. "He wants to have innocent rodents killed." Steeling himself, he fixed his attention on Difatim. "Call off your troops. Tell them not to loot anything. Get the Sapling and leave everybody else alive."

The jerboa snarled, but before he could speak, Sanu pointed the scimitar closer at him. "I know how to use this. Now give the order."

Leaning on his spear, the soldier stooped to meet Sanu's gaze. "You have proof?" Sanu nodded gravely, and the soldier glowered at the noble. "We'll see what Nasalid says about this. You heard the boy. Make the call or I will."

Threatening somebody with a weapon wasn't the military glamour Sanu had dreamed of, but execution didn't sound much better.

30

JAB

Jab couldn't stop the engineers from placing their makeshift bridge over the rubble that hid Jorjim. He shuddered at the possibility his actions might have allowed somebody's death, but the All-Planter judged intentions and Jab never intended to kill him. He hoped his intent to defend himself and save lives would eventually be enough come Pruning Day.

He leapt from his rooftop perch, holding Jorjim's borrowed helmet tight in his tail.

Shattered bits of Mom's prayer rock tangled in his fur. Assuming he survived and procured a new rock, maybe he'd say a prayer in front of the holy Gnaverwood tonight if this siege went well.

Went well. He couldn't believe that thought entered his mind. Rodents were dying.

Jab landed in the street, running toward the onrushing cavalry. Beside Nasalid's honor guard, a detachment of riders split, bound for the Gananhall, while the honor guard approached in Jab's direction. He held the officer's helmet aloft. "I'm a scout! I have information! I have information!"

His shouting almost matched the cadence of the infantry chanting behind him, mopping up the Frenglese soldiers.

The riders at the front of the honor guard slowed, then parted.

Clad in full armor, Nasalid rode to the front. A banner carrier galloped beside him, holding the golden wolf standard high. Nasalid removed his five-feathered helmet.

He didn't gaze upon Jab with a fatherly smile, but relief and uncertainty coursed through the jird's eyes. "Hail, Jab, savior of Rattin." His eyes narrowed and the relief drained from his expression. "Where's Kashdood?"

"Hail, Liberator." Jab's voice caught in his throat, but this wasn't the time for tears. "Kash ... died protecting me. We found out something you need to know though. There are Grovekeeper families living here."

Murmurs rumbled through the soldiers.

"That's not all. There are children here too. Lots of people who could never raise a spear. This isn't a fortress full of soldiers like we thought. It's a city with innocents."

Nasalid urged his horse to face his troops. "Anyone caught looting or killing a noncombatant will be jailed or worse. Ride out to each detachment and spread the news." He pointed to four soldiers, who took off in different directions. Looking back to Jab, he asked, "And what of Lady Marjitay? Or the Sapling?"

"I know where the Gananhall is. I heard rumblings about them not getting along. Get to the Gananhall first. The Sprouter soldiers won't attack you if you have the Sapling with you. They're loyal to Marjitay, but they believe the Sapling can tell the All-Planter to send them to the Droughtlands."

Nasalid leaned forward in his saddle, extending a paw. "Ride with me. We'll speak with the Sapling together. Difatim took a group there, but after believing his advice that you and Kash must have died in the city and we should attack today, I think I'm reconsidering his powers of judgment."

Jab accepted his paw and joined the Liberator in the saddle. Innocent lives would be saved.

Nasalid deserved the title of Liberator.

31

SANU

A true defender knows this paradox: the goal of fighting should be to end the fighting.

- Warrior Maxims

Sanu lowered his scimitar from Difatim's face, and the helpful soldier lowered his spear. Behind them, a fire raged near the residential quarter. Innocents were in danger.

Sanu's gaze fell on Zantiz's corpse. A pitiful porcupine who only saw Sanu as a means to an end. He possessed no warrior spirit, only a killer's, matching his devilbeak. It was a gruesome weapon; the thought of what it could do turned his stomach.

Yet the devilbeak wasn't there, because Difatim clenched the weapon in his tail.

By the time Sanu realized what was happening, Difatim was swinging the devilbeak toward the soldier, but his weak arms made the attack clumsy.

The soldier parried with his spear. "Run, boy. Tell our brothers inside of Difatim's treachery. Save who you can. The Liberator will—"

Difatim's club collided with the soldier's chest, and he slid to the ground, but still breathed.

Eyes wide, Sanu backpedaled and spun around, then sprinted toward the Gananhall. He whistled for Vermitch, and the dutiful horse raced to him, pushing the jerboa noble out of the way, buying him a few seconds in this chase.

A group of mounted soldiers approached. These must be Nasalid's own troops. Sanu glanced over his shoulder, taking in the sight of Difatim chasing him, while the banners of Nasalid himself flew from the approaching horses.

Difatim pointed at Sanu and shouted, "Assassin! He'll murder the Sapling and blame you, Liberator!"

The word "no" lodged in Sanu's throat, but he didn't have time to argue with anyone, even if his childhood hero was on the other side of those horses decorated like an honor guard. Sprinting toward the Gananhall probably didn't scream "innocence" to the new troops.

Sanu didn't care. He needed to get inside.

Save Cladh and the Sapling, stop the other soldiers from looting, and finding the orphans. The Sapling *agreed* with them, for the All-Planter's sake.

The double doors hung open, welcoming the sunset light—close to the time when all the Grovekeepers should stop to pray. Yet if they were fine breaking the fast, who knows what other sacrilege they'd commit in the name of retaking ZelZaytun. Break holy laws to claim a holy place.

Now he really felt like Jab. He rushed inside, where some soldiers kicked over tables and others plucked paintings from the gray stone walls.

A trio of squirrels clad in armor with Nasalid's symbol plodded into the basement where the orphans were. Sanu ran over to them and shouted. "Hey! Kids are in there. Orphans. They'll need medical attention."

The squirrels looked at each other before gaping at Sanu. Some of the battle fury left their eyes and one gave a slow nod. "Thank you," he said.

Sanu knew where Cladh's room was, because she'd told him once. But if she and the Sapling weren't guarded anymore, he knew where she'd be. Instead of checking on Cladh, he ran for the Sapling's quarters. He stopped at the groups of looting soldiers, telling them Nasalid had countermanded their order to loot. Some stopped. Others scoffed and continued.

Sanu didn't have time to persuade everybody. He pressed forward to the back of the Gananhall, through the sanctum, to where the Sapling would be, holed up like a prisoner under Lady Marjitay's hateful eye. As he made for the stairs, a crossbow bolt whistled past his ear, lodging in the stairwell door.

Pawsteps plodded behind him.

Sanu gripped his scimitar, ready for his attacker. The orphans were safe, so nothing would stop him from protecting the Sapling.

32

JAB

- Divine Poetics

Galloping through ZelZaytun's streets, mere blocks away from the holiest spot in the world fulfilled everything Jab had hoped for while growing up. The tree which led to the Walled Garden was here.

Riding through here with Nasalid, finally liberating the great city fulfilled Sanu's dreams—the dashing hero, making his own legends by swinging Dad's scimitar.

Nasalid's honor guard sped toward the Gananhall. Based on the orientation of the front door, Jab realized if the holy area of the building was in the back, all the rodents inside would face the great olive Gnaverwood as they prayed. That wasn't too different from what Grovekeepers did.

As they reached the building sacred to the Sprouters, where their Sapling would be hidden, Difatim limped forward, abandoned by his soldiers. Two corpses lay at his hindpaws.

Difatim pointed behind him, toward a short Sprouter soldier dressed in Lady Marjitay's colors. "Assassin! He'll murder the Sapling and blame you, Liberator!"

Nasalid's horses couldn't all fit inside that narrow entrance, but Jab was faster on hindpaw than all of them since he wasn't heavily armored or burdened by a pack. He hopped off Nasalid's horse, pulling a pawful of crossbow bolts out with his tail and the matching weapon with his paws. Nasalid preferred the lighter crossbow for his troops, unlike the clunky Sprouter variety.

Jab raced inside. "I'll stop him!" Jab wouldn't let anyone destroy the one chance at peace. Saplings were holy to the Sprouters, and if ZelZaytun's Sapling died today, nobody would forgive Nasalid. War would again fall on the city.

The short assassin had a huge head start, but Jab had the fervor of truth pushing him forward.

Nasalid and others shouted for Jab to pull back, warning about the danger. Whatever. Jab didn't care. He'd become heroic like Sanu, brave like Kash, and a protector like his parents. He'd redeem this city and help the Sprouters and Grovekeepers live peacefully together again.

As he passed Difatim, the jerboa smirked. "Don't trip."

Jab hopped over the fallen soldier. Beside him lay a porcupine's body. One look was enough to identify it as Zantiz, which filled Jab with a mix of disgust and pity he didn't quite understand.

Jab sprinted with all his might. He entered the building, where some of Nasalid's advance troops already were. They must have been Difatim's detachment. It looked like they were putting the inside of the Gananhall back together. A trio of squirrel soldiers were escorting crying children up the stairs, as gently as someone could while also carrying a spear at their back. Other soldiers reframed paintings, making sure they were centered, and placed prayer benches back upright. The assassin's lead shrank, as if something had slowed him down while inside.

Jab was close enough to fire. Kash had taught him how to make a running shot. He could end this.

He brought the crossbow in front of him, readying the bolt with a turn of the crank. *Racka-click.*

The assassin neared a wooden door that would likely lead to a stairwell.

Another squirrel. Brown, like him. And not just short, he was Jab's size.

Mid-step, Jab aimed like Kash had taught him. He had to ignore the bushy tail.

Fhwit!

Jab's bolt sailed through the air and *thunked* into the wooden door.

Spooked, the assassin stopped dead in his tracks and whipped around, revealing his face. In the second stretching to an eternity, Jab wondered what kind of heartless beast would become an assassin.

Those eyes, that wild hair: Sanu! No mistake. He'd been alive this whole time—in league with the Sprouters, and Jab had almost killed him.

By the All-Planter, Sanu was alive!

Jab had wanted to live up to his brother's dreams, but Sanu had been in ZelZaytun this whole time, probably calling it Olihort, rubbing elbows with the enemy he'd once sworn to defeat.

Light crossbow clenched, Jab approached his brother, the traitor.

33

SANU

Would you rather have your name remembered in song or return to your family when this ends? That's a decision you must make for yourself, but you cannot make it for your troops.

- General Ironseed's reprimand
to a failed sergeant

Sanu was convinced he'd watched Jab die, but here he was, glaring at him and holding a weapon. So much for Jab being the calm religious one. Sanu's eyes drifted toward the crossbow bolt lodged in the door. His throat tightened, wondering if it were a warning shot or a failed kill shot.

The stranger with his brother's face marched forward. Getting a better look at him, Sanu wondered if this were somebody else; this person wore the garb of a ZelZaytun citizen yet sported a shade of fur darker than Jab's. One other clue suggested this couldn't be Jab for real. Jab would never forgo Mom's prayer rock—the thing always stuck out near the top of his chest.

"Jab?" Sanu had one way to know for sure. "Nasalid's soldiers stopped looting because I asked them. I asked them because I thought that's what you would do. There's a Sapling upstairs sheltering orphans. If we bring him to Nasalid, he will order the remaining Sprouter soldiers to stand down. They'll listen to him. The ones who don't are loyal to Lady Marjitay. Those are the ones who are the real problem."

The grimace shifted to a frown, and Jab slowed.

Another inhale. "Jab, once we get this Sapling, it'll be time to pray. I... would you like to break the fast with me at sundown? I haven't had a chance to pray since they brought me here, and I know even if Nasalid gave the order to break the fast so you'd all have enough energy to fight today, that you wouldn't have."

"You're not a traitor?" Jab dropped the crossbow and ran, tackling Sanu in a hug. "I thought you were dead. I ... watched the fire take you."

Sanu held him tight. "A knight saved me. I thought *you* were dead. I watched you fall." Something tickled his nostrils. "Why do you smell like cinnamon?"

Jab laughed hoarsely. "I bonked my head pretty good, but a scout caught me and nursed me back to health." The lightness left his voice, and a far-off look pierced his eyes. "That scout died, and I couldn't stop it. You won't believe this, but I joined Nasalid's army because I wanted to live your dream for you. And, uh, the cinnamon is a long story."

The brothers broke their embrace.

Now that he wasn't pointing a weapon at him, Sanu could laugh at the idea of Jab willingly joining a fighting force. "I tried to make peace with the Sprouters because I thought it's what you'd do." The mirth drained from his voice and his whiskers drooped. "I guess I failed."

Jab smiled weakly. "So, you aren't here to assassinate the Sapling?"

"No," Sanu replied. "He's a good rodent. Nothing like Lady Marjitay."

Jab scowled like someone shoved a lemon in his mouth. "Did you meet her?"

"Yes. I'll tell you all about how insane that was. But first, can you tell Nasalid I'm not an assassin? I'll go get the Sapling."

Jab pulled away. "I will. And ... I'm sorry I argued with you so much."

"Me too," Sanu replied. "I'll be nicer from now on."

Jab jogged toward the entrance while Sanu opened the stairwell door. Whether Jab's crossbow bolt was a warning or an attack, Sanu appreciated his brother's aim. If he'd been using the heavier Frenglese variety, the bolt might have shattered the whole door.

He bolted up the stairs, quickly reached the next floor, the Sapling's quarters. He whipped the oak door open, testing the limits of his shoulders.

Inside the opulent office, the Sapling sat at his grand oak desk, head in his paws, weeping. The tall rake-shaped window allowed firelight from ZelZaytun to pour inside. Cladh stood beside him, knife pointed at Sanu.

"Not one more—" Her eyes brightened once he finished opening the door. "Sanu!"

The Sapling looked like he'd aged ten years in the few days of his house arrest, but a spreading smile chased away the years.

Sanu stumbled inside. "I've come to ask if you can come downstairs and surrender the city."

Cladh snarled. "Are you kidding me? I thought you were here to rescue us, you—"

The Sapling waved a paw. "Cladh, please. Nasalid is here? In the fur?"

"Downstairs, yes. I'm sorry. The troops here didn't stand a chance. But if you surrender, the good rodents here will listen to you and accept Nasalid."

Pushing himself off the desk, the porcupine rose and approached Sanu. He wasn't wearing the ornate robes anymore. He resembled a regular rodent who forgot how to sleep. "I'm afraid I cannot command as much authority now. When they locked me up here, Lady Marjitay took my amulet."

Cladh stared at her hindpaws. "You don't have to cover for me, Excellency." Her gaze shifted to Sanu, revealing budding tears on her eyelids. "He entrusted it to me and I'm the one who lost it. I should've used this knife on the soldier who took it."

The porcupine sighed. "Cladh…"

Sanu scratched the back of his head. "I know I don't understand everything about Sprouterism, but do you really need that amulet?" Sanu fumbled for an inoffensive way to form his question. "It's not … magic, right?"

"It's a symbol." The Sapling rose from his desk. "And symbols have meaning. This amulet serves as a visible sign of the invisible trust the Arborist placed in me. That trust gets passed to each Sapling, as has been the tradition from Ganan's first Landscapers." He stood beside Sanu in the doorway and placed a paw on his shoulder. "Come, take me to Nasalid. Let's hope he is as compassionate and fair as the stories say."

Cladh sheathed her knife and joined them. "I don't know if this counts as a rescue, but thank you, Sanu."

"Of course." As Sanu led them down the spiraling stairs, he wondered what his meeting with the Liberator would be like, if Nasalid would even accept the saplings words as true without the amulet. Even though it resembled just another pretty acorn, Nasalid would understand the symbolism of authority it carried.

Sanu repressed a sigh. Things were easier when he was following Sir Brouglas and Yagub around. But they were stuck somewhere, maybe alive, maybe dead from dehydration after getting sick from poisoned water.

The memory made Sanu clench his fists. Maybe Nasalid wasn't the one who had that water poisoned. Difatim could've ordered it. He wanted to loot the city and kill innocents.

Yet as Sanu prepared to leave the stairwell, he blinked hard. If the garrison from Castle Kraksnout all died from dehydration in the wilderness, that spared the holy city from more fighting. He wondered if the adults believed that war allowed for cruelty.

Sanu's stomach rumbled, reminding him that fasting had saved his life today. He definitely needed to thank Jab for that.

But first, he needed his brother to help him talk to Nasalid and end the fighting.

34

JAB

What separates rodents from beasts? Our capacity to choose. Tell me, would a horse turn in a horse thief? If a lion killed your brother in the wild, would you call it a murderer? This is among the many reasons we have to thank the All-Planter. Choice.

- Raticenna's collected sermons

As the sun crept closer to setting, the rays of light hitting the colored windows scattered, creating a marvelous rainbow on the floor, surrounded by rows of lit candles and lamps ensconced on the wall. This would be a beautiful place to pray. It deserved preservation. Jab got a better understanding of Nasalid, standing in the doorway, removed from his horse, un-helmeted. A rodent of action *and* peace.

A Liberator.

Jab rushed to him. "Lord Nasalid! That was no assassin."

The jird's neutral expression turned to a scowl. "Difatim," he muttered. "I will deal with him. Who's that?"

"My brother, Liberator. The one I thought had died. He thought I had died as well and Sprouters welcomed him. He got to know the Sapling and wants to bring him to you for a surrender."

"Can he surrender the city though?"

"I'm not sure how their system works. The Sapling and Lady Marjitay are somehow both in charge but don't get along."

Nasalid huffed. "You'd be surprised at how often things like that happen in political affairs. I will accept his surrender. Is that him?" He pointed at the stairwell behind them, where Sanu exited with an older porcupine and youngish hamster. Jab had expected the Sapling to dress like a ridiculous children's doll from the stories he'd heard, but the hobbling figure resembled a grandpa.

"It must be. My brother said he'd get him, and I trust him."

The jird waved for two bodyguards to join. "And I trust you, Jab of Rattin. I look forward to meeting your brother. Join me."

Nasalid strode forward. He glanced around at the art, not lingering like Jab, but absorbing like a respectful outsider. Somebody would shout at him to rebuild this place into a prayer house, but Jab knew Nasalid would never hear of it. He could've drawn his sword, yet instead made a show of giving his weapons to his bodyguards as he approached the porcupine Sapling, the hamster girl, and Sanu.

Breathing deep, Jab stepped between the two groups. "You stand before Nasalid, Liberator of ZelZaytun."

Technically, announcing Nasalid was Difatim's job, but that jerk couldn't be trusted anymore.

Sanu smiled, then turned to the Sapling and the girl and spoke in Frenglese. Hearing those words from his lips felt odd. But one word, or rather name, stuck out. "ZelZaytun."

Somehow, hearing his brother use the invader's language but keeping true to the city's rightful name made everything alright.

Switching languages, Sanu addressed Nasalid. "Hail, Nasalid the Liberator." He looked like he was fighting to hide the smile from his snout at seeing his hero. "You stand before the Sapling of ZelZaytun. Lady Marjitay stole his amulet."

"*Hmpf*. Sounds like her, if the stories are true," Nasalid mumbled. He cleared his throat and stared at the Sapling. "Well met. I'm sorry to hear you were robbed. Seems the Goose of ZelZaytun and you are at odds. Here are my terms. Know I am here to restore the city, not destroy it." His whiskers stiffened. "And I'm not here to negotiate."

Cladh translated and the Sapling nodded. "He's ready to hear the terms," Sanu said.

"First, all armed Sprouters must lay down their weapons," Nasalid began. "You'll tell the

Arborist in Gananshire, and Lady Marjitay will tell the nobles of Freng that Sprouter pilgrims may travel to ZelZaytun unarmed and will be welcomed." Nasalid nodded to Cladh and waited for her to translate before continuing. "Second, if Freng can commit to peaceful pilgrimage and trade, I will allow your vowed religious to take some of the great Gnaverwood's seeds." A measure of stern kindness thrummed in his voice. "I know the olives won't grow in Frenglese soil. We will reserve a portion for Sprouters each year, but the majority of seeds will still grow wild in the sacred grove."

As Nasalid spoke, some murmurs rumbled behind him. Jab understood their disdain. Nasalid would allow something blasphemous to the Grovekeepers in order to maintain peace—somehow wrong and right. Maybe the All-Planter would rather have them get along with the Sprouters.

"All Sprouters who wish to remain on the holy island may. *Peacefully.* Any Sprouters who want passage to Freng may leave without worrying about pursuit."

Behind Nasalid, someone muttered, "Too generous."

After Sanu finished translating, the Sapling replied. "You cannot trust Lady Marjitay. I hoped for a bloodless way to have peace, but I agree to your terms." The porcupine's tired face brightened, "I will make sure every Sprouter in the world knows of your compassion."

Jab's heart thumped. He and Sanu had done it. But as he fought the urge to run to his brother for another hug, he realized this meant nothing if Lady Marjitay disagreed.

The Honking Goose might not be so accepting.

35

SANU

In the Gananhall his friends considered holy, Sanu stared at the man he'd revered, the one who offered a peace so generous one might think he'd lost. Yet Nasalid's soldiers behind him, who should've been cheering, grimaced. Maybe some had come to ZelZaytun hoping to re-enact the decades-old massacre, in revenge for their parents' or grandparents' honor. Perhaps they were salivating over the precious items and artwork surrounding them in this beautiful building that they couldn't loot. So many valuables in the form of precious metals and gems decorated precious paintings. Anybody could steal a pawful and live like a noble.

Sanu and Jab seemed like the only Grovekeepers in the room happy with Nasalid. Sanu guessed his brother was thinking about how Nasalid was following the Divine Poetics somehow. The holy book had rules about military engagement. That much he could always remember. However, he couldn't be sure, since Sanu had changed so much since the battle at Rattin's horns. Jab probably had too. Maybe the brothers had become strangers.

But Sanu's heart twisted for a different reason. While glad ZelZaytun wouldn't flow with innocent blood, he couldn't forgive the reality of the poisoned well. Staring at the imposing figure of Nasalid among grumbling troops, Sanu wondered if that had been carried out by a different rodent. If Nasalid even knew.

Time to test that.

As the Sapling accepted Nasalid's terms, Sanu spoke up. "But what about the well poisoned outside ZelZaytun?" His heart thrummed so hard, he might not even hear the response.

"Poison?" Nasalid's tail flitted against the floor like an agitated broom. "Where?"

Some soldiers murmured among each other, with expressions ranging from surprised to worried.

Nasalid mumbled something to himself, too quiet for Sanu to understand.

Jab heard it though. "Difatim? Nasalid, I'm sorry to say in front of so many soldiers, but he's a traitor. He lied about my brother, saying he was an assassin."

Sanu had heard that name before. "Difatim provoked the Sprouters here by destroying sacred objects in full view of the city guard instead of negotiating."

Every Grovekeeper head in the building snapped toward Sanu.

Cladh stepped forward and spoke in lightly-accented Qawari. "He's not lying. I was there. That jerboa noble insulted and taunted Lady Marjitay's top general. He never tried to negotiate. The lady's retinue all assumed you sent him to insult us."

Nasalid silenced the room with a raised paw. "That is why the troops were so eager to attack. Difatim will know justice. He'll be brought to Lady Marjitay and we'll sort this out. All of you, accompany me. Our scout's brother will lead the way into her keep. We'll enter the palace of the great Mulcher kings of old. Let us all remember the sanctity of that building and keep everything in order. We won't do anything to provoke the Honking Goose further."

The crowd exited the Gananhall. Nasalid ordered one of his honor guards who spoke Frenglese to remain and watch over the children inside. Tightening his tail, Sanu hoped this soldier counted among those who didn't grumble when Nasalid forbade looting.

Exiting the Gananhall, puffs of smoke and ash drifted through the streets, made hazier by the setting sun. Sanu's stomach roared, begging him to break the fast.

Nasalid pointed at the soldier posted to watch the scowling Difatim. "Tie him up. He'll apologize for his insults to the Sprouters."

As the guards shuffled around to bring the traitor beside Nasalid, Sanu hesitated. He didn't want to leave Cladh and the Sapling, but he needed to be with his brother, learn what he'd been doing in Nasalid's camp, share with him about his time with the Sprouters. The idea of Difatim having to apologize for his provocations did little to settle his discomfort, but seeing him in chains shuffling beside the Liberator was a tiny bit delicious.

Defeated Sprouter soldiers were marched through the city, some shouting and others wailing, as Nasalid's troops led them back to camp. Sanu recognized a few of the Sprouters' uniforms. The Kraksnout detachment had arrived—too late and too exhausted to make any difference.

Placing a paw on Jab's shoulder, Sanu stammered a question which came out as nonsense.

Playfully, Jab pushed him aside. "We'll get a chance—"

A pair of soldiers held a chain, pulling two Sprouter prisoners: a beaver and a squirrel. Both were resisting the pull of their Grovekeeper captors. Upon spotting the Sapling, the beaver roared loud enough to catch everyone else's attention.

Sanu's eyes widened.

Sir Brouglas and Yagub, bloodied but alive.

Composure returned; Sanu grabbed Jab. "They are the Sapling's protectors. They can mediate with Lady Marjitay. Jab, they are two of the good ones among the Sprouter fighters here."

Inhaling deep, Jab nodded. "Let's get Nasalid."

Running alongside his brother for the first time in a month, Sanu bounded through the mess of troops surrounding the Liberator, the conquering hero of ZelZaytun. Seeing his hero should've been the high point of his life, but knowing his brother was alive was so much more important to him now. Jab not pointing a weapon at Sanu helped also.

"Nasalid," Jab called.

Strange to hear the name at that volume without the cadence of the chant he'd heard earlier.

"Nasalid!" Jab persisted.

The jird, who Sanu now realized was the same age as their father, turned his horse to face Jab, accompanied by a still scowling Difatim.

"We need those two prisoners for the negotiation," Jab said. "The beaver and squirrel."

Sanu caught up and stood beside Jab. "They're loyal to the Sapling. They don't fear Lady Marjitay. The beaver has some pull with Frenglese nobles. They can testify to the poisoned well."

Nasalid pointed to one of his soldiers guarding Difatim. "Retrieve those two and bring them before me."

Difatim spat on the pavement. "You're taking the word of a child?"

"Two," Nasalid corrected. "I wish I could have earlier. Their hearts are purer than ours, and that's what it'll take to truly protect this city and the All-Planter's Gnaverwood." He snapped his gaze to the rest of the soldiers. "Is that not our great wish, men? To keep the All-Planter's grove? To secure a place in the Walled Garden for ourselves and our families? I am here for that, not slaughter. I hope you can say the same for yourselves."

The grumbling stopped, but Difatim scoffed. Sanu hoped somebody would smack him.

Brouglas and Yagub were brought over, and the struggling stopped.

The beaver knight stammered something in Frenglese, too hoarse to comprehend. Yagub looked like he was one drop of moisture away from dropping dead of dehydration.

As the sun dipped to the top of ZelZaytun's remaining walls, Sanu reached for his water flask. He could now break the fast. But as he readied to drink, he saw his suffering friends. Taking care of the needy first was more important.

He approached Yagub and held the flask to his lips. After letting his surrogate older brother drink, he did the same for Sir Brouglas, the beaver who risked his life to save him.

Between the two of them, they'd finished the flask, but Sanu felt full.

"After negotiating terms with us, the Sapling is safe," Sanu said. "So is Cladh. We're escorting them to tell Lady Marjitay to back down."

"She'll never agree to that," Yagub croaked.

Brouglas coughed out a laugh. "We ... see will ... about that. Make her ... agree ... I can."

Nasalid's ear twitched. "Your skills in our language are impressive, Sir Beaver. Inform us what you can do. I have a way to force her to agree as well."

Sanu's eyes drifted to Nasalid's scimitar attached to his saddle, noticing the details on the handle for the first time: the same checkered design as Dad's.

36

JAB

- Divine Poetics

The Gnaverwood stood so tall it periodically blocked the sun, creating a giant sundial around the island, and obscured the moment's sunset. Jab should've been sitting with a meal right now, but the soldiers who were supposedly his rodents-in-arms had eaten and drank today for the sake of the siege, frenzied for revenge over a lie.

Breaking the fast allowed the soldiers to make a surprise attack. That saved Grovekeeper lives and increased Nasalid's negotiating position. And Sanu's kindness proved him to be the ideal Grovekeeper, even if he hadn't kept his snout in holy books since he could read.

Jab smiled at his brother, hoping Sanu would be proud of him.

At Nasalid's order, the retinue continued toward the ancient Mulcher Kings' palace. Jab and most of the other soldiers averted their eyes from the great tree, as the city wasn't officially won yet, but a few in their group stole glances at the sacred trunk, only to immediately slap a paw over their eyes.

It was too magnificent to behold. Too sacred to comprehend and too upsetting knowing their parents and grandparents were killed over access to it.

Nasalid strode at the front, flanked by body-guards, with Jab and Sanu directly behind. Difatim shuffled forward, slumping in his chains. Sanu's Sprouter friends, at Nasalid's insistence, rode on loaned horses, sipping on Nasalid's own water flask—an act which also garnered a few scowls. Behind them, the Sapling and Cladh rode on another borrowed horse, and Nasalid even apologized for not providing one earlier.

The dark thought rose in Jab's mind. Had Nasalid been a secret Sprouter this whole time? Jab pushed the idea away. Being nice to one's friends and countryrodents came easily. Showing compassion to a defeated enemy took greater virtue, which the Liberator had.

Exhaling his misgivings, Jab allowed him-self to appreciate the architecture leading up to the Mulcher kings' great palace. Stone arches loomed over them, all carved to resemble intertwined tails from rodents of all species. This was originally intended as a sign of their global dominion, which Grovekeepers reinterpreted as a sign that the All-Planter loved rodentkind in its entirety. Jab wanted to think that Sprouters would appreciate the same symbolism, but he wondered if Lady Marjitay and her ilk came closer to the original interpretation and intent. Jab clenched his fists. He wasn't being kind. He needed to emulate his generous brother.

Once they reached the palace's double gates, two horrified guards crossed spears and shouted something in Frenglese. Lady Marjitay must've sent her tougher soldiers out already—straight into the spearpoint or a prisoner camp.

Brouglas the beaver knight said something to the guards, and the Sapling rode forward, nodding.

Sanu nudged Jab and whispered, "Sir Brouglas said the Sapling surrendered and we need to see Lady Marjitay. If they lay down their weapons, Nasalid will treat them kindly."

The two Sprouter guards glanced at each other and passed their weapons over to one of Nasalid's soldiers. They knew the city had been lost; Jab hoped the nobles inside would have that same understanding.

Nasalid dismounted, facing his soldiers. "I have four Sprouters and one traitor I must bring inside, along with the savior of Rattin and his brother. That is eight, including myself. I will only take ten of you inside." He counted off ten soldiers, who joined him at the entrance. "Two of you, comb the streets and ensure all prisoners in camp are given the appropriate offers and sustenance. The rest of you: guard the entryway. No massacres today."

The thirty-two remaining soldiers of Nasalid's honor guard patted their chests and about-faced.

Inside the Mulcher Kings' palace, a tableau of interreligious and cultural exchange was illustrated in the mismatched artwork. As Jab marveled at the three faiths' shared history, mythology, and core beliefs, symbolized in different ways in clashing art styles, he understood what ZelZaytun needed to be.

Sanctuary for all.

Stronghold for none.

He saw Nasalid with new eyes: the Liberator, not just for Grovekeepers, but all rodentkind. Everyone who worshipped the All-Planter would see Nasalid for who he was. Choosing equality and compassion over supremacy upset only the spiteful soldiers and corrupt ones like Difatim. If what Sanu said about the Sapling rang true, they'd have a wonderful partnership. A new age of peace, trade, intellectual exchange, and—

Racka-click. Racka-click.

It came so quietly, Jab wouldn't have noticed if he didn't have Lady Marjitay's goose and crossbow symbols glaring at him. He placed a paw on his brother's wrist and held a finger over his lips.

Racka-click. Racka-click.

Someone was loading a crossbow. Training with Kash taught him the tell-tale grinding.

They were approaching a branching hallway, and the winding gears gently echoed against the stone.

Jab's eyes widened and his hair stood on end. He pushed Sanu to the floor, and jumped up, using his tail as a spring for extra height. He knocked over the soldier who held Difatim's chain, and tackled Nasalid.

Fhwit-chunk!

The crossbow bolt flew through the hall, sailing over the downed Liberator and into the Sapling beside him—the bolt's force knocked him to the floor.

With a gasp and grunt, the Sapling, greatest hope for peace, grasped the projectile lodged in his ribs, while seventeen other rodents gasped.

The hamster shrieked as blood splashed onto her. "No!" In a rush, she knelt beside him, and tugged at the bolt lodged in his chest.

Sanu ran to her, pushing through the small crowd of soldiers.

Racka-click.

"Shields!" Nasalid called. "There's an assassin in here with a crossbow." With a *whoosh*, ten shields clanged together, making a metal barrier. "Get the Sapling back to camp," Nasalid ordered. "Take him to Maimon—cover your retreat."

Jab's blood boiled. Lady Marjitay must have had a few of her better guards stay behind. This whole place could be booby-trapped.

The squirrel, who could've been Kash's cousin, placed an ear over the porcupine's chest. "He's not breathing."

Racka-click.

Brouglas muttered something in Frenglese, and Sanu translated for Nasalid. "He said this is typical of Lady Marjitay. If we can keep cover, he'll lead us to the throne room."

"If she means to fight," Nasalid hissed, "I doubt she'll wait for us there. She can also escape behind us if there are hidden passages around."

Fhwit-chunk!

A crossbow bolt rammed against the shield covering Nasalid's neck, denting the metal. The hamster girl wept over the dead Sapling, muffling the noise of the collision.

Sanu crawled forward. "Nasalid, if the Sapling is dead, everything he said is meaningless."

Nasalid's whiskers drooped. "His surrender is invalid."

Difatim chuckled, but Sir Brouglas silenced him with a stare.

The jird took a deep breath. "Jab of Rattin, you heard the crossbow loading. I trust you to find the source. I owe you my life."

"I can figure out where it's coming from. But I'll need some help." Jab extended a paw to his brother.

37

SANU

Strategy wins battles. Give a fool a fancy weapon and he'll hurt himself. A superior tactician can win bare-pawed.

- General Ironseed's reprimand
to a failed sergeant

Sanu's twin asked for help from him, maybe for the first time in their lives. Though terrified, Sanu accepted Jab's paw.

"Let's stop that crossbowman," Sanu said. If Dad were here, he'd mutter something like "famous last words."

Racka-click.

Jab's ears perked and rotated. "Do you know your way around the palace?"

"Not as well as I should," Sanu replied. "I've been afraid of Lady Marjitay."

Beside them, Nasalid's whiskers drooped.

Sanu had just disappointed his hero. "But I know someone who does." Sanu faced the beaver knight and squirrel squire, his protectors and friends. "Jab will hear the shooter loading, but we'll need a warrior to protect us as we go forward."

Brouglas tapped his armor. "This is useless against a heavy crossbow."

"We need someone who can wrestle them and get the weapon free," Sanu said. "You can use my scimitar too."

Yagub glanced at Cladh. "She is now the highest-ranking religious official here. If you want the truth to get out, she must be protected as if she were the Sapling."

Racka-click.

Cladh's ears stiffened and she wiped her eyes. "I'm not some precious weakling for you to protect. I'll tear out Lady Marjitay's teeth myself for what she's done."

Something about her grit made Sanu's heart thump faster. He avoided the urge to nudge his brother and translate everything.

Collecting herself, Cladh shook her head. "*But* I'm the one who can testify to the world that Marjitay killed the Sapling and refused peace. So somebody does need to protect me." Her voice hardened and she stuck a stiff finger in front of Sanu's snout. "But if you think for one second you can throw your life away, you've got another thing coming."

Racka-click.

"Get down!" Nasalid shouted.

Fhwit-chunk!

Another bolt dented the shield protecting Nasalid.

"No more talking," Sanu said, switching languages. "Jab, lead the way."

Jab signaled for the soldiers protecting Nasalid to part their shields, and he slithered out of the opening, followed by Sanu, then Brouglas and Yagub.

After the shields returned to their position, Jab inspected the damage to the shields and the broken bolts on the floor. "What's down the left hallway?"

Yagub's tail stiffened. "The barracks and weapons cache."

Brouglas nodded. "Let's go!"

Racka-click. Faster this time.

Jab's ear rotated toward the sound. "Got it. Look behind stuff." Jab sprinted toward a statue of an ancient Mulcher king. "There!" An ornate green dress—the kind Mutarra and Qala would ridicule—was visible between the statue's legs, gliding over the figure's boots like a phantom.

Sanu mirrored his brother's zig-zag across the tile, running toward the assailant, the one who had murdered the Sapling. Dress whooshing around her, Lady Marjitay stepped out from behind the statue, ornate crossbow loaded.

"Don't move," she hissed, pointing her weapon at Jab.

No. Not again. *No!* Sanu had already lost Jab once and he would not let it happen again.

"She said don't move, Jab!" Sanu called. His brother probably didn't need a translation.

Fhwit—

Jab rolled to the left, hugging the floor. The bolt slammed into the tile, shattering a piece. Better ancient stonework than Jab's skull.

"Murderer!" Sanu screamed. "You're not worthy of the throne. Give up!" His throat burned from screaming and running, but he urged himself forward to match pace with his bounding brother, who was in much better shape than a month ago.

Racka-click.

She'd already affixed the crossbow's loading mechanism for the next attack. Perhaps, with all the time she should've prepared the city for an attack, she was only preparing herself.

Racka-click.

Brouglas and Yagub lumbered behind. The poor rodents must have been whiskers away from death.

"I'll defend this palace with my last breath," Lady Marjitay said. "Sir Brouglas, I order you to kill these boys."

Racka-click.

Jab was almost to her, and she detached the loading mechanism. Sanu banked left as the so-called Protector of Olihort aimed. They were so close. She wouldn't miss at this range.

Sanu recited the sunset prayers, drawing on his brother's strength to push forward. Marjitay's finger looped around the trigger.

No!

She and Zantiz had already taken so much. Sanu wasn't about to lose his brother again.

Leaping like Jab had before, Sanu dove for her hindpaw. Jab, catching Sanu's gaze, dove for the opposite one. The brothers pulled at her ankles, forcing her to stumble.

Fhwit-chunk!

Sailing through the air, the bolt hit the ceiling, lodging itself in the wooden rafters, bringing a rain of splinters down. The hateful mole rat fell backward, dropping the crossbow with a *clang*.

Sir Brouglas and Yagub caught up to them. Chuckling, the beaver knight grabbed the weapon and brought it to his mouth.

Yagub smirked. "Lady Marjitay, by the authority of the interim Sapling Cladh, you are under arrest. Resist, and my knight will bite through your crossbow. You know what they say about beavers and imported wood."

She scowled at them, whiskers tangling with her plummeting eyebrows. "You can't arrest me. I'm the Protector of Olihort."

Brouglas chomped into the handle with a crunch that echoed through the hall. "Call the ZelZaytun." He flashed a splintery smile to Sanu and Jab.

"The battle is lost," Yagub added. "You refuse to surrender, and more rodents will get killed."

Sanu released his grip on her ankle. "Nasalid is prepared to offer a fair deal. You'd do well to take it. Stop the fighting. Return to Freng with some dignity."

"Olihort is my home," she hissed. "I'm a woman of the rodents."

Brouglas took another bite of the crossbow, then spat out some pulp.

"You're not," Sanu replied. "But I've seen someone who is." Sanu caught Jab's pleading eyes. Looking over the defeated noble, Sanu nodded to Jab and switched languages. "It'll be alright. We've won."

38

JAB

Jab and Sanu were the only rodents in the holy city to truly break the fast that night, which made the spread of cheeses all the sweeter. Eating in the throne room in the palace of the ancient Mulcher kings with Nasalid made it even more delicious, as if it brought out the nutty aromas.

The Liberator offered Lady Marjitay a seat at the table and refused to sit upon the throne himself. Both actions stirred an odd grumble from the soldiers, but she ignored his offer and slumped in the corner under the watch of Yagub and two of Nasalid's soldiers.

Word came from camp. All the Sprouters' weapons were confiscated, and the prisoners were given a meal and a chance to wash. At Nasalid's insistence, Maimon and Yark joined them in the throne room. Since Lady Marjitay refused to dine with Nasalid, Brouglas and Cladh sat in her place, with two chairs where the mole rat once had a large ornate one for herself.

Jab was awed at the scene. He and his brother had helped Nasalid liberate ZelZaytun. To honor the late Sapling, Cladh and Brouglas both agreed to Nasalid's terms.

Rattling her chains, Lady Marjitay sprang up. "I do not surrender the city!"

Nasalid leaned over, placing his bite of cheese back on his plate. "You're welcome to join the negotiations."

After Yagub translated, she spat on the floor.

Sir Brouglas said something to Nasalid, and Sanu translated. "The nobles of Freng don't like her. But they also need to know she is unharmed for political reasons. Get her out of here. Dump her on some other nobles. We will testify that the Sapling died by her arrow. She'll never manage so much as a tavern, let alone rule a city."

Nasalid listened with rapt attention, then turned to Jab. "You said you met Grovekeepers practicing in secret here. There are also thousands of innocent Sprouters here. They must be terrified of what I'll do to them. Putting myself on that throne will certainly cause retaliation. Damouscus is my capital."

Jab lifted a finger. "I have an idea."

As eyes settled on Jab, he swallowed his cheese to give himself an extra moment to think. No pressure here. Just figure out what to do with the holy city. After a gulp of water, he cleared his throat. "The Frenglese who conquered ZelZaytun spilled lots of blood. I even saw a few spots on the stonework in the streets that were still dark, as if no amount of rain would ever clean them. Roses and blood are the same color. Maybe your troops could clean the city streets with rosewater? It won't remove all the stains or bring anyone back from the dead, but it would show the world you don't want to repeat history and want to go forward in peace."

Maimon chuckled. "Good with a crossbow, brave, wise, and devout. You could've used more advisors like him, Nasalid."

Eyes closed, Nasalid nodded slowly. "It's unfortunate Jab is too young to rule this city. Is there anyone in Rattin who would govern fairly?"

Jab scratched the back of his head. "Maybe more than one rodent could rule the city? Maybe Grovekeepers, Mulchers, and Sprouters could share it?"

A few soldiers groaned, but Maimon, Cladh, and Brouglas leaned closer. Nasalid held out a paw to Maimon. "Thoughts?"

Maimon tugged on his beard, saying, "They would still need to recognize your political authority, but such an arrangement could be made. There are pockets of local Mulcher families in the smaller towns, and you already have a few Sprouters who support your rule." He indicated Brouglas, and Cladh, and made a show of avoiding Lady Marjitay to point at Yagub.

Nasalid leaned toward Cladh. "How will the Arborist in Gananshire take to these arrangements?"

"Hard to say," she replied. "If the right princes get in his ear, he might order an attack. But if you allow pilgrims and trade as you say, justifying retaliation would prove difficult, especially if you allow Sprouters to live here peacefully."

"I will," Nasalid said.

Brouglas shifted in his seat and spoke, and Sanu translated. "There are princes who will want to retake the city for the glory of it, even without the Arborist's backing. If Prince Ridgerd hears about this, he might raise an army."

For a flicker, Nasalid smirked, as if he found the prospect of matching wits against Prince Ridgerd in battle amusing. "I won't have any more bloodshed around the sacred tree. He and any other princes may come here as pilgrims, unarmed. The real issue is how to convey this message to the Frenglese nobles. I cannot trust the mole rat over there to speak plainly, but I cannot keep her here."

The Liberator faced Sanu and Jab. "Brothers of Rattin, squirrels of unquestioned bravery, the two of you understand the importance of ZelZaytun to both sides." His gaze settled on the brothers. "Jab, you know how *I* think and Sanu knows how Sprouters think. I'll send you both in my name with a peace offering. Sir Brouglas, I also need a titled Sprouter knight who will speak plainly. I cannot send two children across the

Great Sea, as brave as they are, unchaperoned. Will you escort them and corroborate? I'll supply you with an entourage to keep a tight watch on Lady Marjitay. I'll compensate you well and will have a place for you in my capital at Damouscus when this is over."

The beaver crossed muscled arms over his chest and spoke in their language. "Two conditions. One, you let Yagub join me if he chooses. He grew up here and can attest to your good treatment of the local Sprouters. Two, somebody has to give me this recipe."

"Agreed on both accounts," Nasalid replied. "And the two of you?" he asked Sanu and Jab.

Jab nodded toward his brother. Their parents' way to the Walled Garden would no longer be blocked. "The prayer warden of Rattin, Miai, would be a good candidate to watch over ZelZaytun. I can't speak for Sanu, but I'll go."

"Me too," Sanu said.

The days since the surrender had been a blur. Fewer soldiers grumbled about Nasalid after the fighting abated. Some members of the Kraksnout garrison even volunteered to join in washing the streets with rosewater.

Now that ZelZaytun was back and truly open to Grovekeepers, Jab welcomed his brother and their town into the Gnaverwood's grove. A single root rose from the ground which could have functioned as another layer of wall for the city. It may have even held better against Nasalid's siege engines than the stone. Jab introduced Miai to Nasalid, telling the prayer warden about the possibility of having a paw in managing ZelZaytun, to make it a city of peace for all rodentkind.

Banners flew overhead and the aroma of fresh cinnamon sheltercake scented the air.

Sanu brought Mutarra and Qala over to Jab, and he gave both sisters a hug.

"Mutarra," Jab said. "We have a present for you."

Qala scoffed. "A bigger present than letting the whole town into the city?"

"Not just them," Sanu said.

"Look!" Jab pointed at the open gate, where more Grovekeepers poured through. These were from the towns, villages, and cities that dotted the island, from all the shattered realms of what was once ruled by the Five Princes, now united under Nasalid's empire.

"Nasalid invited everyone to make a pilgrimage," Jab said.

Within seconds, the crowd swelled from a few dozen to a few hundred, and a happy clamor outside the gate suggested thousands more were pouring into the city, though it never felt crowded.

As the four friends had to huddle together in the growing crowd, Qala smiled. "Are you two really hitting the open sea?"

"We're leaving tomorrow," Sanu said.

Jab reached for Qala's paw. "Yeah, and I wanted to make a proper goodbye." His eyes bulged. "To Mutarra." Sweating, he turned to the younger sister. "Remember that present we mentioned?"

The girl nodded. "Out with it!"

Sanu and Jab reached into their tunics and produced her two lost dolls. "Sorry to keep you waiting."

"Yeah," Jab chuckled. "We got a bit sidetracked."

Mutarra squealed, hopped in place, then squeezed them tight.

"You both held onto them?" Qala asked.

"It didn't seem right *not* to," Sanu said. The bulging crowd made them huddle closer. "And Jab wanted to impress you, of course."

Jab coughed hard and Qala rolled her eyes. "H-hey," Jab said. "It's almost time."

The shade darkened.

Noon.

Miai, aided by Yark, sang the call to prayer, which rang out through the sacred grove.

Together, the assembled community cheered, then gazed up to the Gnaverwood. They all knelt together, praying in the manner they were supposed to.

The tree was magnificent, a glorious pillar of life rising to the Walled Garden. The creases in the bark ran up like rivers, and the sunlight through the leaves cast a pale green glow over the ground. His parents were right: it had been worth the wait.

Nobody here would truly mind sharing a piece of this with their Sprouter or Mulcher neighbors.

This was what the All-Planter had wanted and told them to work for. So much of the Divine Poetics had injunctions to hear, and this swelling ecstasy of fellowship resulted from rodents actually listening.

They didn't have to avert their eyes from the Gnaverwood anymore. They didn't have to be angry or fearful anymore.

A new flag flew over the holy city of ZelZaytun.

Former enemies, now neighbors, could be brothers.

United.

ZelZaytun may be safe for now, but someone across the Great Sea will not be happy to learn about Nasalid's conquest. Look out for Book 2 of the Grove Guardians series, coming soon! Or if you need more rodent madness in another part of the Great Sea, check out the *Ghosts and Iron* series!

BOOK CLUB QUESTIONS

1. How did believing something untrue change Sanu and Jab's perspectives?

2. Nasalid also believed something untrue: he thought Rattin and ZelZaytun were only military outposts. How do you think things would have played out differently if he'd known the truth from the beginning?

3. Who was your favorite brother and why?

4. Sanu and Jab weren't the only "brothers divided." Where did you find other groups or individuals in the story who should've been close but weren't?

5. Sprouters believe eating the olives is a way to respect the tree, but Grovekeepers believe eating them disrespects the tree. How do you

think they can both be correct, even though their views are opposite?

6. Sanu and Jab met some helpful friends and dangerous foes on their journeys. Which side character was your favorite and why?

7. Why do you think it was important to see characters who were kind and cruel on both sides of the conflict?

8. Sanu believed that Jab was the smart one, but he found that he had a gift for learning languages. Jab believed that Sanu was the strong one, but he became athletic and a good scout. What are some things in your life you never thought you'd be able to do because of what you believed about yourself?

9. What was your favorite part of the book?

10. What are your predictions for when Sanu and Jab sail to Freng?

AUTHOR BIO

PC is a fantasy and science fiction author from the Great Lakes region of the USA. Fantasy has been a deep love for PC, who grew up on Star Wars movies and reading the Redwall series. The Star Wars novels along with fantasy greats like Brandon Sanderson, C.S. Lewis, and Tolkien are constant sources of inspiration and wonder. PC loves taking his daughters to the zoo, and the occasional sushi or taco date with his wife. With the help of historians and martial artists, PC tries to blend real historical elements with some great rodent action in his stories. Tune in to the Radio Freewrite podcast to hear original works by PC. Visit PC's website at authorpcnottingham.com and sign up for the newsletter for updates and exclusive content!

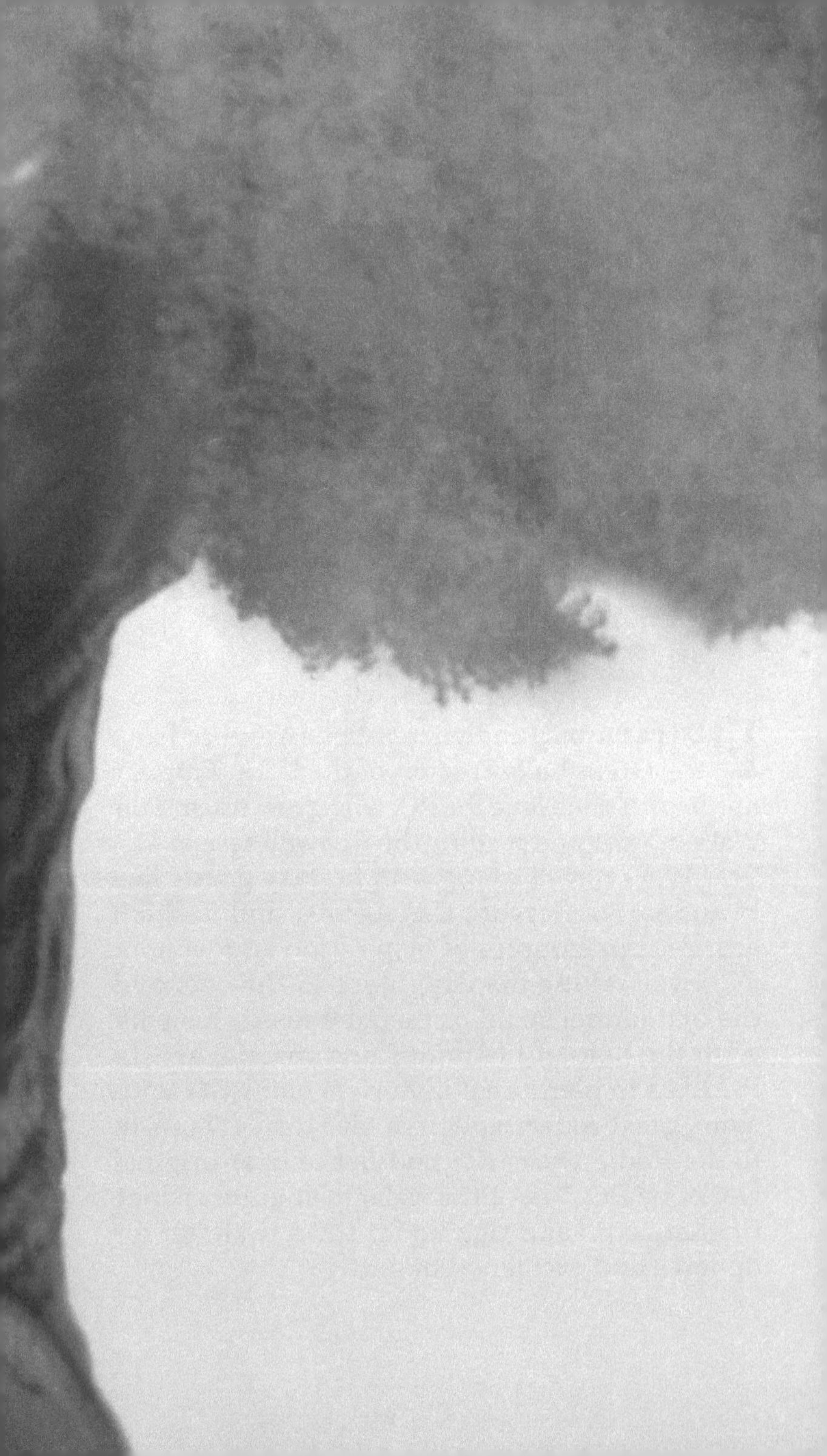

Discover more at
4HorsemenPublications.com

10% off using HORSEMEN10

www.ingramcontent.com/pod-product-compliance
Lightning Source LLC
Chambersburg PA
CBHW032358310726

48973CB00007B/2075